A CHRISTMAS IN CONNECTICUT

A CHRISTMAS IN CONNECTICUT

EMILY FRENCH

For April,
my dear friend and best supporter.

Pictures of perfection make me sick and wicked.

— JANE AUSTEN

CHAPTER 1

*C*laire Bennett continued to stare at the website for several more minutes. She looked again at the pictures of the house: a 1930s white clapboard cottage with black shutters and a red front door. All the windows had small panes of glass, the chimney constructed of smooth river rocks, and the entire property enclosed by a white picket fence. There were pictures taken in each of the different seasons, but it was the ones taken during the winter that had caught her attention...and her heart. Mounds of white snow on each side of the neatly shoveled walkway, a large pine wreath hung on the front door, and dark green spruce trees flanked the house. It was, as her mom would have said, "cute as a button." She decisively hit the "Book It Now" button and leaned back in her chair. She felt exhilaration and anxiety all wrapped in one emotion shoot through her body as she took a deep breath. Little did she know she had just changed the course of her life forever.

"A little help, please."

Claire looked over her shoulder. She'd been so engrossed in thought that she hadn't heard the front door.

"Sure—sorry, I didn't hear you." She took some of the packages from her best friend's arms.

Emmy Parsons heaved the rest of the bags onto the kitchen island. "It feels like the friggin' north pole in here. Why is the a/c set so high?"

"Because I'm roasting in all of this," Claire said, motioning to the wool turtleneck sweater and tall leather boots over jeans she was wearing.

"It's like 90 degrees out. Why are you wearing all of that?"

"I was going to write the turkey post while you cooked it...I need to *get into the spirit* of the season, get my...creative juices flowing." Claire waved her hands around her head as she said this. "So, give me just the thumbnail sketch of what you'll be doing."

Claire and Emmy had met in college. They were matched up as roommates and had been best friends ever since. In her senior year, Claire had an assignment to create a blog in one of her marketing classes. Emmy had helped develop the idea of a lifestyle blog. She'd had tons of great ideas, which, when combined with Claire's talent for creative writing and stunning visuals, made it a success. A *big* success. To their shock, the blog took off. After graduating, they made it their full-time profession. *City Meets Country* had been earning them a living ever since.

Emmy had placed the large plastic bag containing the turkey in the sink and rinsed it. "First, I brined it for forty-eight hours, and then after rinsing and drying it thoroughly, I'm going to stuff it with aromatics, truss it, butter it and season it before putting it in the ov—"

"Hold up, you're going too fast," Claire said as she wrote with one hand and held up the other. "Explain brining again."

"Really? We do this every year, Claire; I can't believe that none of this ever sticks."

It was established early on that Emmy was the one with

the talent to bake, cook, create, plant, knit and craft amazing things; Claire had a way with words and could write in a way that drew readers into their lifestyle-world as well as create eye-catching images for the blog. Their talents fit together like two puzzle pieces.

Emmy was painfully shy and had made it crystal clear that she didn't want her face anywhere near the website, she'd insisted that Claire be the face of the blog...arguing that Claire was the photogenic one with the outgoing personality and that no one would be interested once they knew that the person who created half the blog was someone who, in her words, "ate their feelings." Claire had told Emmy more times than she could count that she was "curvy" and that the brand would benefit with her face behind it. But Emmy wouldn't budge. It was a deal breaker. So, Claire was the sole face and name of their blog.

"Well, I can't...so remind me what exactly brining is..." Claire continued to write in the notebook next to her computer. "Oh, and by the way, I did it." She looked up from what she was doing and met Emmy's eye.

"The whole cottage in Connecticut thing? Oh my god... you're kidding. Are you sure? I mean, wow, kind of scary." Emmy had her arm up to her elbow inside the turkey, stuffing the cavity with onions, carrots, and celery. Her brown eyes grew dark as she looked at her friend.

"Not kidding. And yep...I'm sure. I really can't stay in L.A. for Christmas...it's tough enough all the other days." Claire looked down at her lap, biting her bottom lip.

"Will you be okay all alone? I'm afraid you'll be lonely," Emmy said. She'd washed her hands and had come over next to Claire, putting her arm around her. "You know you are more than welcome to spend Christmas with us."

Emmy still lived with her parents. Partially because Los Angeles was phenomenally expensive, but mostly because

Emmy was very close to her family and was having a hard time leaving the nest. She lived in a granny cottage on their property. It had everything she needed—except for a full kitchen, which is why she did all the cooking for the blog at Claire's.

"Thank you—but I really need to do this. I can't be in L.A. for the holidays." Claire's face brightened as she took Emmy's hands into hers. "But—you could come *with* me. It's got two bedrooms; it would be so much fun to do it together."

Emmy smiled back at her. "I'd love to, Claire...I know we'd have fun together and we would get a lot of content for the blog. But you know, I'm not sure how many more Christmases Nona will be with us."

Nona was Emmy's grandmother, who lived with Emmy and her family. She and Emmy were super close. In recent years, Nona's health had declined. "I just hope that you'll be okay three thousand miles away in Connecticut." She hugged Claire tightly.

"I'll be okay. I promise."

Emmy returned to preparing the turkey as Claire turned back towards her computer. "I see myself bundled up in scarves and holiday sweaters, drinking hot chocolate and cranking out some *amazing* content." She typed away, glancing up to see Emmy shoving the large bird into the oven.

I will be okay. Right? She told herself she'd have to be, because staying wasn't an option. Her parents were killed in a car crash earlier in the year. The sudden loss of them had been brutal on Claire. She was an only child and didn't have siblings with whom she could grieve with. It had felt as if someone had cut her open and slowly crushed her heart with their hands — the pain was *that* intense.

As time went by, it had gotten easier. She'd moved out of her shoebox apartment in West Hollywood and into her parents' townhome in Santa Monica. She'd hardly changed anything; getting rid of their things felt like erasing the memory of them. She had eventually come to grips with their deaths and got by okay on most days, but Christmas would be difficult. She let out a deep breath and continued to focus on writing. Soon she was finished writing *City Meets Country's* latest post.

TACKLING *That Thanksgiving Turkey*

I know how intimidated many of you city girls are by the idea of roasting an entire Thanksgiving turkey, and you're probably wondering whether you can serve a Thanksgiving charcuterie board instead. I'm here to tell you not to worry; it can be done! Not only can you do it, but it can be fun as well! Yes! Fun! If possible, I highly recommend finding a turkey farm. You can even find them in urban areas without having to drive too far. Not only will you be getting the freshest possible turkey, but the time spent out at the farm will rejuvenate your soul and give you all the feels! The farm I visited was just as cute as it could be. Gentle rolling hills dotted with adorable happy turkeys strutting around, complete with a red barn and even an overall-clad farmer. It's an experience not to be missed. So, take a deep breath. You've got this! Click on the link for the step-by-step recipe. Gobble, gobble!

CLAIRE LEANED back in her chair while Emmy read over her shoulder.

"A *turkey* farm? Have you ever *been* to a turkey farm?" Emmy gave her one of *those* looks...a dubious one.

"Well, no...not in *person*...I did an Internet search on organic turkey farms for inspiration."

Emmy continued to give Claire *that* look.

"What?" Claire asked.

EMILY FRENCH

"Don't you think that's going a bit too far?"

"Not at all. You know as well as I do all blogs embellish... we're selling a *lifestyle.* It doesn't mean that *we* live it all, exactly to a tee; a little creative license sparks people's imagination." With that, she closed her laptop, signaling that the conversation was over.

"Okay. Well, I'm going to leave for a bit. The turkey will be okay for a couple of hours. I need to go stay with Nona; she's home all alone. I'll be back...just don't touch it." She raised her eyebrows at Claire as she grabbed her purse.

"I won't, don't worry."

* * *

CLAIRE WENT through the mail in her hand. There was lots of stuff addressed to her parents. She made two piles: one for mail that was to be kept and the other for the recycling bin. She came across a glossy over-sized flyer with a picture of a handsome man in a suit holding a "sold" sign in front of a house. *Zachary.*

Her heart caught a bit at the sight of him. He looked handsome...*and* sexy, with a small confident smile on his face. He and Claire had been together for two years. It had been a good match, or so she'd thought at one time. Something changed after her parents died. And it wasn't something that Claire could articulate clearly. All she knew was that despite having a boyfriend, she'd felt alone. Something had been missing when she was needing the most from him.

Although she'd been the one to end things, the sight of him still gave her heart a tug. Since he plastered his face on every bus stop bench and billboard around town...and was now in her mailbox...Zachary was another reason she needed to leave for the holidays. She tossed the flyer into the recycling pile.

She returned to her computer and pulled up the listing for the cottage in Connecticut. Just seeing it filled her with warmth, as well as something else, something she couldn't quite put her finger on. Just the sight of the little house filled her heart with good feelings.

When Claire's mom heard about the lifestyle blog she and Emmy had created, she couldn't wrap her head around it. Claire could barely boil water and had never shown an aptitude for crafty projects. After explaining each of their roles behind the enterprise, her mom had replied, "It's exactly like *Christmas in Connecticut*," and had promptly sat Claire down to watch the movie. The story was about a young woman living in Manhattan, a modern-day *Sex In The City* type, who writes a successful magazine column about homemaking, even though she can't seem to boil water either or sew a button on a garment. It culminated in hilarity when a handsome young soldier was invited to spend Christmas with her at her non-existent Connecticut farmhouse.

Claire had loved the movie, and she and her mom watched it at least twice every Christmas season. The memories of watching it with her mom, huddled under a cozy throw blanket and drinking hot chocolate, even if it was one of those hot Los Angeles December days, gave her heart a pang. Her current thought process was that a change of scenery would make the memories less painful. She smiled, tracing her finger along the image of the cottage on the screen. "I'm going to have a Christmas in Connecticut, Mom." Her eyes welled up with tears ready to spill down her cheeks as she let out a shuddered sigh.

CHAPTER 2

*J*ack rubbed his neck and looked at the numbers in front of him. He'd been looking at them for hours and had made no progress. In college he'd studied business and had never come across any accounting method that resembled his dad's bookkeeping. Jack leaned his head back and stared at the ceiling. *It's going to get easier, right Dad?* He let out a deep sigh. It made him feel better to imagine that his dad was listening. He missed him. A lot.

"Hey there Jack, why the face?" The older man removed his faded Red Sox cap and rubbed the top of his head while his crinkly eyes closed, before focusing themselves on Jack. "What's troubling you?"

Hank Olson was a childhood friend of Jack's father, Harry. They'd gone to school together, played college baseball together, and served in Vietnam together. And when they both returned to River Falls after serving, Harry took over the family hardware store and Hank had tagged along. He'd been working there for over fifty years now.

"Think it's time for a new one?" Jack nodded his chin up at Hank.

"A new what?" Hank asked, replacing the cap on his head.

"A new cap. That one's gotta be a thousand years old by now." Jack chuckled.

"Are you kidding me? Never. That's when." Hank shook his head. "Haven't I told you the story of how I got it?" the old veteran asked.

Only about a hundred times, Jack thought.

"Carlton Fisk handed me this cap right after batting practice before game six of the '75 World Series." Hank was getting worked up from the memory. "Fisk had been hitting the ball so badly he pulled the cap right off his head and shoved it in my hands, saying he needed to change his luck. He changed his luck alright and hit the game winning home run that night in extra innings." He headed out of the room. "When am I getting rid of it, pfft...gonna be buried in this thing," he muttered under his breath as he left.

Jack smiled and turned his attention back to the books in front of him. He had moved back to River Falls just before his father's death six months earlier. He'd just finished his tour in Afghanistan and had been submitting applications to various businesses in the Hartford area, where he'd planned to move once someone hired him. His father's death had meant that either he or his sister would need to take over the hardware store that'd been in the family for three generations. His sister Beth wasn't an option, she was due in just a few weeks with her first child. So, it had fallen on Jack to take over. It wasn't what he'd wanted for himself, but here he was.

But now he was wracking his brain, trying to figure out where the business stood financially. From Jack's view, the business was losing money and had been for a while. Amazon and the nearby Walmart hadn't helped matters. His dad had been a people person more than a businessman. He was the type to allow customers to buy on credit, the only

9

credit being that he knew them, often resulting in large unpaid tabs. That particular business model wouldn't be sustainable going forward. He needed to figure out how to save the business…that is, if he *could* save it.

* * *

CLAIRE PULLED the rental car into the driveway and studied the house in front of her. It *was* the same house; it was just that she was expecting it to be surrounded by fluffy white snow. Instead, leaves covered the ground, lots of them. Which when mixed with the recent rain had turned into a soupy, leaf-sludge. At least as far as she could tell from the streetlamps above, the sun had set hours ago. It was dark. From what she could see of the house, it was adorable. She couldn't wait to get inside.

She grabbed two of the four suitcases from the car and slung her laptop bag over her shoulder, making her way to the door. Once inside, she fumbled around for a light switch, finally flooding the entry hall with light. She dropped all her bags and looked around. From the entryway she could see into the dining room, the kitchen, the living room and down the hall to the bedrooms.

She flipped on the wall switch for the living room and let out a little squeal. The focal point of the room was an enormous fireplace with a white mantel flanked by two wall sconces. Throw pillows in different shades of blue, covered the cream-colored couch. Two cream colored slipper chairs stood on each side of the fireplace; soft blue blankets draped over their backs. Positioned in the middle, a painted blue coffee table sat. Built-in bookcases, stuffed with books and knickknacks, stood on each side of the fireplace. A beautiful area rug nearly covered the hardwood floor. It was downright cute and cozy. Claire was already picturing herself sitting in front of a roaring fire, writing incredible material for upcoming blog posts.

She walked through the dining room into the kitchen. It was cute with a capital C. The cupboards were a light robin's egg blue, the counter tops were polished white stone, brass pendent lights illuminated the huge butcher block island. *It's too bad I don't really cook. But it will definitely help gin up my imagination when writing cooking posts.* She smiled and snapped off the light. After retrieving the last two bags from her car, she investigated the main bedroom.

Claire beamed from ear to ear when she caught sight of the room. She admired the iron headboard, the bed layered with fluffy white and navy quilts. The two side tables and dresser were the same blue as the kitchen cabinets. Brass lamps flanked each side of the bed and a large, brass framed, ornate mirror leaned against one wall. "I made the right decision," she said aloud just before plopping down on the bed. It was even softer than it looked. She spent the next hour emptying some of her suitcases before deciding it was time for bed.

After changing into her pajamas and brushing her teeth, she fished her phone from her purse and read the text message that had just come in:

Emmy: Call me as soon as you're settled...I can't wait to hear about it!!!!!

Claire phoned her friend.

"So...is it what you imagined?" Emmy's voice was bubbly.

"Yes, and more. You have no idea, it's such a different world than L.A., it's so quiet for one thing. Oh...and the house is adorbs! I'm already inspired, I'll probably be able to write months' worth of content here."

"That's awesome, Claire. You deserve some happiness after the year you've had."

"Thank you, sweetie. I'll miss you," Claire said quietly.

"I'll miss you too...hey, I'm dying to know...did you meet up with Zachary?"

Zachary had contacted Claire a couple of days before she left. He'd left a voice mail saying he wanted to see her...just to "talk." Except she and Zachary never "just talked" without ending up in bed. Sex had been the glue that joined them together. They had chemistry that worked. *Really* worked. But after Claire's parents had died, the rubber met the road, and the sex alone could no longer hold the relationship together. Zachary hadn't understood her depression. "Snap out of it," or "pull yourself up by your bootstraps," he would say, whatever the hell *that* meant. He bristled when she told him she'd seen a psychiatrist who'd prescribed anti-depressants for her. He acted as if not having the internal fortitude to just "get over it" without professional help was a weakness. It had been a deal breaker for Claire.

"I didn't. As tempting as it was, and as badly as I need to have sex again," she sighed aloud, "I told him no."

"Good girl, I'm proud of you. Maybe some long walks in the crisp New England air will relieve that tension."

Claire doubted a walk would do the trick.

"Keep in touch and text me lots of pictures," Emmy said.

She and Claire talked for a few more minutes before hanging up. Claire snuggled down into the bed and read a book until she felt tired and snapped off the light. Except her mind wouldn't turn off. She was thinking about Zachary. Specifically, *sex* with Zachary. The sex had been outstanding. It was the one thing she really missed. Just thinking about him in bed got her revved up. Maybe a good orgasm was what the situation called for, so she could relax and get some sleep.

She snapped the light back on and swung out of the warm bed. She rooted around in a suitcase she hadn't yet unpacked. *Where is it?* Finally, her hand wrapped around the vibrator before pulling it out from under some sweaters. She'd tried to hide it just in case her bag needed to be inspected at the airport. She didn't need some TSA agent giving her a raised eyebrow and judging look. Claire snapped the switch on and...nothing. She snapped it back on and off several times and still...nothing.

"Damn it."

She silently added batteries to her list of things to pick up the next day and glumly got back into bed...alone.

* * *

"You're a lifesaver, Jack. Thank you."

Jack stepped into his sister Beth's home, handing her the small brown bag.

"Where's Tyler?"

Tyler was Beth's husband of four years. He worked for a big pharmaceutical company out of Boston, splitting his time between working from home and being on the road either to Boston or elsewhere.

"Business trip to Austin. Can I get you a bowl also?" Beth yelled out from the kitchen.

"Nah...I'm good," Jack replied.

Passed out on the couch was Beth's Scottie dog, Archie. The dog opened one eye, let out a snort, and went back to sleep.

Jack walked back into the kitchen and sat at the counter. "How many weeks are you now?" He'd swear she was having twins, though he was smart enough not to say that out loud. Beth had practically torn off the head of the last person who'd asked if she was carrying twins.

She sat down next to him. "Thirty-two weeks...the finish line is in sight." She took a bite of her ice cream, her eyes practically rolling back in her head as she ate it. "I don't know why—but it can only be Belgian chocolate…nothing else will do. Luckily Marty keeps it stocked." Marty was Martin Larson, the fourth-generation owner of the only market in town, River Falls Grocery. "I just didn't have the energy to put on real shoes over my swollen feet *and* try to squeeze behind the wheel of the car." She pointed with her elbow down to her feet, which looked like loaves of bread in her socks.

"Is that much swelling normal?" Jack asked.

"I don't know. I have an appointment with Doc Wooden tomorrow morning. I'm tempted to wear slippers when I go." She ate the last bite of ice cream.

"Christmas is going to be hard this year, isn't it?" Jack asked. It would be their first holiday without their dad. Thanksgiving had been rough, but Christmas was the holiday where their dad would truly be missed. He had always embraced the season wholeheartedly and pulled out all the stops to make it magical. He even dressed up as Santa Claus when they were kids. Beth had shared the news of her pregnancy a few weeks before he died. He had been ecstatic about becoming a grandpa.

Beth reached out and touched Jack's sleeve. "I want to do everything in my power to honor Dad. I want to embrace Christmas just as he would have…I refuse to have it be ho-hum because we're sad he's not here. Let's make it special, Jack. Between you, me, and Tyler, we can do this. Margie always brings a dish…maybe I can get her to do more."

"She can barely see anymore…I'm not sure that's such a good idea, I'm pretty sure I saw her having a conversation with her trash can the other day."

Margie was the eighty-eight-year-old widow who lived across the street. She didn't have any family close to her, so when her husband died ten years ago, they'd always invited her over for Christmas dinner.

Jack looked around the kitchen. "The remodel really turned out nice."

"It did. I was hesitant to change it at first, since it was the kitchen we'd grown up in after all, but it was time." After their father passed away, Beth and Tyler had moved into the family home. Their dad had had little to leave them, just the house and the hardware store. Jack and Beth were on title to both. They hadn't worked out anything official, but for now Jack was fine with her and Tyler living there. It felt like the right thing to do.

"Let's coordinate about Christmas and come up with a plan. I want to fill the house with as much Christmas spirit as possible. I've been bookmarking some blog posts for inspiration. Let me get my iPad and I can show you some of what I had in mind," Beth said.

Jack watched as she waddled to the living room, returning with her iPad in hand.

"I looooove this woman." She shoved the screen in front of Jack's face. "Isn't she adorable! You need a woman like this, Jack."

He stared at the woman in the photo. She had shoulder length light brown hair, big brown eyes, some freckles on her nose and a beautiful, slightly crooked smile. "Yeah, she's cute," Jack responded as he continued to look at the image.

"Remember those loaded chocolate chip cookies I would send you? I got the recipe from *her* blog."

"Those were good...some guys were offering to buy them from me." Jack remembered the chocolate chip cookies loaded with bits of crunchy, salty pretzels...a combination that tasted like heaven.

"Any hoo...she's got loads of great Christmas ideas in here."

"What's her name?" Jack asked. He wasn't interested in

the holiday ideas…just the woman. She had that rare combination of cute and sexy all in one.

"Claire Bennett. The name of the blog is *City Meets Country*. She has the *cutest* ideas…and the *best* recipes. I'll start making a list of projects and menu items." Beth's soft curls bounced as she excitedly talked to Jack.

"You're right…let's do Dad proud this year," he said. He kissed his sister on the forehead and then headed home.

Jack couldn't get the cute brunette off his mind. He hadn't had a girlfriend when he'd left for Afghanistan six years earlier, which meant he didn't have one now either. The hope was a new life in Hartford would offer opportunities to meet someone. In River Falls, he knew practically everyone, and either the women weren't his type, or if they were, they weren't available, which kind of sucked because Jack really missed not having a partner. He also missed having sex. Yeah…it sucked. He drove home, the image of Claire Bennett firmly planted in his brain.

CHAPTER 3

*J*ack was taking inventory of the stock in the back room. It was becoming clearer every day that his dad's business acumen had been non-existent. He still wasn't sure whether he could save the store or not. If he could get it into the black, enough to provide a livable wage for himself and some profit for Beth, he'd be okay with spending his life in River Falls. It wasn't what he imagined he'd be doing with his life, but he'd never imagined his dad not being around. He'd only been seventy-four, and was healthy, at least he seemed so. Jack had pictured his dad running the store for another ten or fifteen years, but the universe had other plans, and Harry had suffered a massive heart attack and was gone "like that." One moment he was here, the next moment gone forever.

"Cute out-of-towner just walked in…you should go check 'er out," Hank said, walking into the storage area, pointing his thumb back towards the store. He had a sly grin on his face and a gleam in his eyes. He always told Jack whenever an attractive woman walked into the store, acting as an unofficial wingman.

"Oh, okay," Jack replied, bemused. "What makes you say she's an out of towner?"

"She's wearing a Dodgers' cap."

Hank was right. No one from River Falls would be caught dead in a Dodgers' cap...it was Red Sox or nothing. But just the mention of the Dodgers' cap took him right back to Afghanistan. He'd overseen a group of soldiers, and one of them, private Robbie Martinez, had been a huge Dodgers' fan. When he wasn't wearing his combat helmet, he had that damn baseball cap on. Jack's heart felt as if it was made of lead as it sunk in his chest at the memory of Robbie. He'd watched as the car Robbie was in was blown to bits by a roadside bomb. It was the only man he'd lost, but it was one too many and it haunted Jack. He shook himself back into the present. He looked at his watch. "Okay, I'll come man the register while you take your lunch."

Jack walked out to the front of the store and spotted her instantly. It wasn't too hard. The Dodgers' cap was only the first clue that she wasn't from around here. The second being the ridiculous shoes she had on; they appeared to be clogs. With ice in the forecast, anything that wasn't firmly attached to your foot could be deadly if you walked on a stretch of black ice. She was cute...and had nice curves, Jack thought as he admired her from the side. She was standing in front of the display of batteries. Her nose wrinkled as she examined different sizes, seemingly weighing them in her hand before returning them to the display. He returned his focused to the balance sheet he was working on.

* * *

Claire stood in front of the display full of batteries. Stupidly, she hadn't bothered to check what size the vibrator required before popping into the hardware store. She was *that* desperate to get it up and running. *Claire, you're a ding-dong.* She *could* go back home and check, but she had so many other stops to make…if she could only make an educated guess as to the size needed. The old, grizzled guy who'd asked her if she needed help had left, and a young, *very* attractive guy had taken his place behind the register. Claire tried discreetly to steal glances at him while she continued to inspect the batteries. He had dark blond hair, a chiseled jaw with a couple of days' worth of stubble on it, and friendly eyes. She was admiring the muscles from his biceps straining through his plaid flannel shirt, the sleeves were rolled up and revealed sexy forearms. She began to feel a bit flushed and lightheaded. To steady herself, she leaned against the display. With a loud crash, the entire thing went over, with Claire on top of it.

"Are you okay?" Mr. Biceps had come rushing over and was holding out his hand for her to grab.

Oh my god, how embarrassing. "I'm fine…but your display isn't." She got up with his help and surveyed the mess. "I'll help clean it up," Claire said, motioning to the mess of batteries lying everywhere, the display was reduced to a heap of cardboard.

"Don't worry about it, we were going to get a new one anyway."

"You were?" She looked at him with a smile.

"No. I just didn't want you to feel bad." He gave her a smile back that melted her entire core. Up close, his light blue eyes grabbed her. She could feel her cheeks start to flush again.

"What are you trying to find?"

"Um…I was just," she felt her heart speed up. *Think Claire. Think.* "Um…just batteries for my…my flashlight." *Good save!*

"Easy. What size are we talking about?"

Claire was trying not to stare at his incredibly sexy lips. "What?"

"What size? Are we talking key chain size? Or a big heavy-duty mag?" He looked at her.

"The *size...of my flashlight?*" she replied as she continued to stare at him. Her face was now beet red. "Um...something in between?" She squeaked out.

"You could always bring it in. That way you'd be sure to get the right battery for it." He stood in front of her, his hands—*big manly hands*—rested on his jeans that were snug against his body.

"Bring it *in*? I...uh...I think I'll just write the size down and come back." She looked into his eyes...*damn sexy eyes.* She watched as his expression gradually changed.

"I know you...you're *her*," he said excitedly.

"Her—who?" Claire replied quizzically.

"The blog...*Country Meets City*," he said, pointing a finger towards her.

"*City Meets Country*, actually. Yeah, that's me. Claire Bennett." She knew their blog was popular, and *occasionally* someone in L.A. would recognize her, but a guy...in a small New England town recognizing her? What were the odds?

"Right, *City Meets Country*." He smiled as he crossed his arms across his chest. "My sister loves your blog. She used to make one of your cookie recipes and send them to me while I was in Afghanistan. Loaded chocolate chip."

"Those *are* good. That's so sweet, thank you."

"I'm Jack Wilson," he said as he took her hand. As soon as he did, Claire felt a sensation race through her body at the touch of his warm hand around hers.

"As in Wilson's Hardware *Wilson*?"

"Yeah—it's a family business...it's been a part of River Falls for a long time."

They stood quietly for a moment. Jack nodded down to her clogs. "We're expecting ice to form later today."

She looked down at her shoes before looking back up at him. "And?"

"Well, you might want something more secure. I'm not sure those would stay on if you hit an icy patch of pavement."

"These? I'll be fine...my toes grip to keep them on...plus they're lined in shearling, totally warm. Well, I better get going...sorry again about your display." She grabbed her purse, that was lying on the ground. "I'll be back...with the battery size," she said as she fled the store.

"Bye," he'd called out to her as she slipped through the doors and into the fresh air.

Once she was back in her car, she sorted her thoughts. *God, he was gorgeous.* Even though the temperature was only 30 degrees, Claire grabbed some papers from the glovebox and fanned her heated face. *Really gorgeous...and damn sexy.*

"Jiminy Christmas. What happened here?" Hank was pointing to the scattered batteries and destroyed display.

"Country...city...looking for batteries," Jack murmured.

Hank's brows narrowed as he stared at Jack. "What? Are you *okay*?"

"She...uh...just...it fell," Jack said as he nodded to the mess.

"Did Dodger cap do this?"

Jack was thinking about Claire. There was something about her. She felt familiar already, and not because of the blog. She was adorable and sexy as hell. He couldn't stop thinking about her. He looked up at Hank, who was surveying the damage and nodded his head.

"Where are we going to put the batteries now?" Hank

asked as he picked up the completely crushed display from the ground.

"Don't know. I'll think of something," Jack murmured. But all he could think of was Claire.

* * *

CLAIRE HAD JUST FINISHED her shopping at the only market in River Falls. The selection had been high quality, if not limited. Not that she'd really been paying attention. All her brain cells were focused exclusively on Jack and his biceps. She couldn't stop thinking about what they would look like out of that shirt, or how'd they feel wrapped around her body. She had her arms loaded down with two reusable shopping bags filled to the brim with groceries and some household items. She was busy rooting around in her purse for the keys with one hand while the other held onto both bags. She smiled again at the thought of him. How adorable he was, being all concerned about her clogs. Pffft...she'd worn these through three days of Coachella...a little cold weather wouldn't be a—

Just as she'd approached her car, she'd stepped on something slippery. For just a brief second, she thought she was going to be okay...it felt a bit like ice skating, albeit out-of-control ice skating, but suddenly her feet went out from under her, the bags flew from her grip, she was momentarily airborne before coming down with a thud on the pavement. *Shit.* She heard the unmistakable sound of a clog making contact with the hood of a car followed by a "What the *hell?*" in a gruff voice in the distance.

"Are you okay?"

Claire's eyes were closed, but the familiar voice caused them to fly open. It was Jack. Again. *Oh my god...he's going to think I'm an idiot who can't stand on my own two feet.* "I'm fine," she squeaked out as she used his outstretched hand to pull herself gently off the ground. "Nothing that some Tylenol and bourbon won't fix."

He narrowed his eyes at her.

"I'm kidding," she said. "Kind of."

"Where's the other one?" Jack asked as he motioned to her feet. One foot still had a clog attached to it, the other only had on a pink sock adorned with white bunnies munching on carrots.

Claire silently pointed with her chin across the parking lot where a heavy-set man in an orange hunting vest was eying the hood of his truck and scratching his head at the presence of Claire's clog lying atop it.

"I got it." Jack jogged over to the truck and grabbed the shoe, saying something to the guy before jogging back over to Claire. "Here," he said, handing it to her.

"Thanks," she replied. "Did it leave a dent?"

"Nothing that wasn't there before, no worries." He helped gather her groceries that were scattered about. He held up a frozen box of mac & cheese and another of home-style meat-loaf. "You eat these? Really?"

"What…don't you ever eat frozen meals?" She eyed him with a look of incredulity on her face.

"Well, yeah, but I don't know how to cook."

"And neither do—" An alarm bell went off in her head before she could finish what she was about to say. It was blasting *don't say it Claire* with big flashing red lights.

He was looking at her quizzically and had momentarily stopped picking up the groceries, waiting for an answer.

"And neither do I *feel* like I can cook very well in an unfamiliar kitchen." She smiled to herself. *Phew. Good save.*

"Because I just read your blog 'farm to table meals in under thirty-minutes.'" He continued to stare at her.

"Well…like I said, right now I'm completely unfamiliar

with the kitchen…so I just need some alternatives while I get acclimated."

He nodded as he resumed retrieving her items…some of which had rolled under the car. "You know, Jenny's Diner is an excellent alternative. She makes great soups. You can buy them by the quart to-go…or any of the other menu items. Have you eaten there yet?" He stood up with her bags in his hands while she unlocked her car.

"Not yet. Sounds good though."

"What are you doing for lunch tomorrow? We could meet there. I'll introduce you to Jenny—I'm sure she'd be excited to meet you—we can have lunch; I'll fill you in on everything you need to know about River Falls."

Claire had gotten into her car and was putting the key in the ignition. She looked at Jack as he leaned against her car door, his blue eyes practically hypnotizing her as she continued to dream about what he looked like out of that lumberjack shirt.

"Sure," was all she could get out.

"Great, I'll meet you there at noon." He closed her car door and watched as she backed up…giving her a quick wave and a gorgeous smile. Her entire insides had turned to putty. *Did he just ask me out on a date?*

CHAPTER 4

*C*laire finished putting her groceries away before filling up a large bag with ice and propping herself up on the couch with her laptop; the bag of ice soothing her sore back. Jack was obviously reading up on her through her blog. She needed to get a handle on what kind of person he was imagining her to be. She found the post she was looking for and quietly read to herself.

*FARM TO TABLE **meals in under thirty-minutes!***

Okay...I get it...many of you have written to me asking how in the world is it possible to work all day and come home energetic enough to cook a meal? Easy, I say! Don't take the quickest way by settling for fast food when there's a better and just as easy alternative. My first word of advice is to read my post from last year: Sunday Prep-day. While the guys are watching the game, you can get a jump on your game by prepping veggies for the entire week. Seriously, it's a game changer. But, even if you haven't done your veggie prep, there is still no excuse for giving up and calling that bucket of chicken you picked up at the drive-thru, dinner. Click the link at the end for twelve delicious recipes using fewer than ten ingredients...all of them fresh... to make a meal fit for the queen that you are, in under thirty-minutes. Now go kick off those heels, take off that bra, pour yourself a glass of wine and get cooking.

CLAIRE CRINGED as she read the post, picturing the image of her Jack must have. Obviously one of a super confident and skilled woman who had her shit together enough to prep a week's worth of food on Sunday instead of lazing around in sweats, which is how Claire usually spent the day, although she could manage the bra-less and drinking wine part with ease. She popped a frozen entrée into the microwave and called Emmy.

"So, it's a date?" Emmy asked after Claire relayed everything that had happened.

"I'm not sure. Kinda doesn't sound like a date," she said as she stuck a steaming bite of mac and cheese into her mouth. "I mean...if it had been *dinner*, then yes...definitely a date... but *lunch*? That sounds too close to 'I'm just being friendly' territory...*right?*"

"Maybe. So how hot is he?"

"Oh my god hot...like burning hot...but in a quiet way, not a 'look at me' way. He's solid...the type of guy that would protect you in a disaster, type. You know what I mean?"

"Uh huh...and he works at a hardware store?"

"Yeah, it's a family business. I got the impression he's running the place."

"Uh huh."

"What's with all the 'uh huhs?'"

"I don't know, Claire. It's just kinda crazy...you just got there and now you've met this guy that you're meeting for lunch...do you think you'll be safe? Do you have your pepper spray?" She could hear the concern in Emmy's voice.

"Of course I'll be safe. This is small town USA...looks like the back of a postcard...not crazy L.A. where the person next to you could be a whack job. He's solid. I can feel it. Besides...it's lunch at a diner, not a meetup in a dark alley."

"Okay. Maybe you're right, maybe it's just a small-town friendly kind of gesture."

"That's what I'm afraid of," Claire said.

They continued to chat. Claire relayed all the charming parts about River Falls and how much she adored the cottage. After they hung up, she contemplated what Emmy had said...it probably was *just* lunch. Which was too bad because Claire wouldn't mind it being a bit more than that.

* * *

JENNY'S DINER was just catty corner to the hardware store. Anything you needed in River Falls was all within a cute two-block radius. Most of the buildings were brick with canvas striped awnings over store fronts. Jenny's was black and white over gold lettering on the big picture window that looked out onto the main street.

Claire pulled the door open and stepped inside. The most amazing smells greeted her, she closed her eyes and inhaled deeply. It smelled like home. The space was made up of comfortable looking booths, and a counter to eat at. She quickly spotted Jack back in the corner. He stood up and walked towards her...like a gentleman.

"Hi," he said, helping her out of her coat, before hanging it up on a coat hook on the wall behind them.

"Hi," Claire replied as she slid into the red leather booth. She couldn't help but notice how well Jack filled out today's flannel shirt. Being around him made her a bit lightheaded. She smiled. "Thanks for the invite...it smells heavenly in here."

"Right? The food is great. I probably eat here at least three or four times a week, and Hank, the older guy at the store, I'm pretty sure he eats every meal here. It's easy, being right across from us." He nodded towards Wilson's Hardware store.

Claire nodded in agreement.

"What brings you to River Falls?" he asked as he looked at her with those sexy blue eyes that made her get that funny, fluttery feeling in her stomach.

"I uh…just needed a change of scenery for the holidays." She looked at him across the table.

"Change of scenery from what?" He said this gently.

"Oh, well, from memories." She sat quietly, and Jack didn't push her to elaborate.

"Hey Jack, back so soon?"

A cheerful woman with her hair piled on top of her head and an apron wrapped around her waist looked at him, a pad of paper and pencil in her hand, waiting to take an order.

"Yep…can't get enough of this place. Jenny…this is Claire. She's from Los Angeles and is renting the Drake cottage."

"Nice to meet you, Claire. That's an *adorable* place. After Dolores passed, her kids kept it and decided to rent it out… I've seen the renovations they made…so cute. I hope you like it there."

"I do, and you're right…it's charming."

Jenny took their orders, a grilled ham and cheese on sourdough with a cup of tomato soup for Jack and a grilled chicken and root vegetable salad for Claire.

Claire looked over at Jack…there was something comforting about him…something safe. The next thing she knew, she was spilling out details of her life to him.

"My parents died earlier this year." She looked down at her hands wrapped around a mug of tea.

"Oh, Claire, I'm sorry."

She glanced up at his face. The concern was genuine.

He reached out and put a hand on hers.

"I know it's been almost a year and I should start to put it behind me, I just—," she said.

"*Who* says you should feel anything other than what you're feeling? Everyone grieves differently, Claire. I know what you're going through."

She looked him in the eyes as he spoke.

"My dad died six months ago. He had a heart attack and instantly was gone. I was shocked. He'd been there just the day before and next thing I know, I'm getting a call from Beth that he had died. It was jarring to my whole being…and there's no one way that you're *supposed* to feel other than what you feel."

Claire now reached her hand across the table. "I'm so sorry Jack." Her heart ached as she saw sadness wash over his face. They sat quietly for several minutes, not an awkward silence, but one of just being still.

Jenny broke the silence when she arrived with their food. Jack was right, it was delicious. Claire actually moaned out loud when she tasted hers. "This is *great*," she said as she put another bite of the tender chicken in her mouth.

Jack had his mouth full and just nodded his head. "I told you it was good," he said after swallowing.

They continued to eat their lunches together. Jack told her all kinds of interesting details about River Falls. The town was incorporated in 1835. Only about 9,000 people lived there and there were many buildings on the National Historic Register.

"Do you enjoy living in a small town?" She asked him. They'd finished their lunches, and neither seemed in a hurry to leave.

"Yes…and no…but mostly yes."

"What do you like about it?"

"I like the sense of community…everyone knows each other, and we help each other out in times of need. The entire town mourned my dad's passing. It really helped Beth and me a lot, not to mention that they fed us for months. It was nice. I imagine you don't really get that in Los Angeles."

"No. Not really. You really only have your own circle of friends and family…maybe a neighbor or two. But there's so much more."

"Like what?" Jack asked.

"Well…for starters, there are about a gazillion restaurants to choose from. Tons of awesome food from other cultures, anything from Korean to Ethiopian. It really is a melting pot, which makes it a pretty interesting place to live despite its shortcomings."

"Yeah, I get that. River Falls is definitely not a melting pot by any stretch of the imagination. It's pretty much a one note town. I can see how variety would be nice."

"Other than it being just a big ol' bowl of vanilla, are there any other drawbacks to small town living?" She admired his face as he thought about what she'd asked. He was handsome in a quiet and rugged way…a way that made Claire's heart beat faster.

He was quiet before looking up at her. "It's been hard to meet someone special."

She could barely swallow the golf ball size lump that had settled in her throat.

"It has?" she croaked out. On the outside, she was trying to remain calm, but on the inside, she was doing somersaults and a happy dance. *Maybe he's single!*

* * *

"You're officially the best brother ever." Beth gave Jack a big hug, swinging her pregnant belly to the side.

"Should you be out of bed? Doesn't bedrest mean resting in bed?" Jack watched as his sister scurried around the kitchen, putting the groceries he'd picked up away.

"I'm allowed to be up for brief periods of time for 'necessary activities' whatever the hell 'necessary' means. She grabbed the ice cream from one of the bags, along with a spoon. "What are we going to do about Christmas now?" she asked as she ate straight from the carton.

"Well…we'll figure it out. Make a list of what needs to be done and I'll see if I can figure out a way to tackle it. But the last thing I want is for you to worry. You need to be taking care of yourself and my little nephew."

Beth smiled at him. "I'll say it again, you're the best brother, Jack." She gave him a kiss on the cheek. She turned to go down the hall and stopped and turned back around. "By the way, Jenny said you were eating with some cute out-of-towner today." Her eyebrows arched up, waiting for a reply.

Another thing to add to the list of what he didn't like about living in a small town: everyone knew your business. "It was nothing…really." He looked at his sister. "Funny thing…you won't believe this, but it was Claire Bennett."

Jack saw confusion on Beth's face. Claire's name, out of context, wasn't ringing a bell for her.

"You know—from *City Meets Country*, *that* Claire Bennett. She's staying in River Falls for Christmas."

"*What*? You're kidding! Oh my god!" Beth shrieked. Jack could practically see the wheels spinning in her head. She looked up at him and began to open her mouth. Jack knew *exactly* where she was going.

"No. No. No. I'm not doing that." He was shaking his head and putting his hands up.

"But Jack, this is a sign, a *good* sign…we want a Christmas that honors Dad, I'm confined to bedrest, and *who* happens to

31

show up in our town? None other than the most talented person in the world at creating homey, festive holidays! Jack, you *have* to." Beth was pleading with him.

"I'll think about it...but you need to go back to bed. I'll put this all away." He shooed her back down the hall to her bedroom. "When's Tyler back?" he called out.

"Not for another three days," she hollered from the bedroom.

"I'll walk Archie for you until he's back."

The dog was asleep in his tartan plaid bed in the kitchen but popped his head up at the sound of his name and the word "walk." He looked expectantly at Jack.

"C'mon Arch...let's go." Jack quickly put the rest of the groceries away and took the dog for his evening walk before checking on Beth and locking up the house behind him. He gazed up at the full moon in the sky and the chorus of stars around it. Another good thing about living away from the city, the night sky was amazing. He smiled and got into his truck and drove home, feeling happy for some crazy reason he didn't quite understand.

CHAPTER 5

"Okay, I guess this 'ell work for now, at least until the new display arrives." Hank placed the last container of batteries on the shelf by the register.

"Yeah, I think it's fine." Jack's attention was not on the batteries though, it was only on Claire. He'd tumbled around in his mind what Beth was suggesting. It was too crazy of an idea, not to mention a *complete* imposition. Claire was in River Falls to escape memories of holidays past. Jack was pretty certain helping his family get their act together for Christmas wasn't on her agenda. He heard his phone ringing. *Beth.*

"Hey Beth, everything okay?" He'd been by earlier and walked Archie and checked on her. She'd bombarded him with ideas for Christmas, hinting again about asking Claire to help.

"I'm fine. Did you see my text? I sent you a list of things we need to do for Christmas."

We? And *need?* Jack was pretty sure that *we* meant him and Tyler...and he already knew Tyler would not be much help.

"No, kinda busy here at the store, but I'll look at it when I get a chance. I promise."

This seemed to appease her, and Jack was able to extract himself off the phone. He pulled up the text and his mouth dropped open slightly as he read through her list:

* **Outdoor holiday lights.** *Easy, check.*

* **Freshly cut Christmas tree trimmed with adorable yet upscale ornaments, maybe even two trees.** *Trees...check. Not sure whether they'll be adorable or upscale, but ornaments, sure. Check.*

* **Holiday wreath for front door.** *Sounds easy enough. Check.*

* **Beautiful gingerbread house centerpiece for dining room table.** *Not happening unless we can make it with graham crackers frosted onto milk cartons.* He was fairly certain that wasn't what Beth had in mind.

* **Buche de noel (aka yule log).** *Uh...all kinds of nope, unless he could get one from the bakery...maybe.*

* **Brined and roasted fresh turkey.** *Ugh.* The turkey Beth made for Thanksgiving was more like jerky. *Not sure brining is going to help.*

* **Fresh cranberry sauce with oranges and cinnamon.** *Try to talk her into the canned stuff.*

Jack read the rest of the list and suddenly felt overwhelmed and all alone. It was clear to him, that Beth wanted a picture-perfect Christmas. Shoot, so did he, but they'd need to be realistic with her confined to bedrest. He'd try to talk to her about it.

He looked up when he heard the jingle of the store's door. It was Claire. He couldn't control the smile that spread across his face. She looked adorable in a pompom topped knit hat, jeans that hugged her curves, and a soft blue sweater.

"Hi," he said.

"Hi," she replied as she walked up to the register. "I'm sorry again about the display." She motioned to the batteries now in bins by the register.

"No worries." Jack rolled up the sleeves of his shirt. "So, what size do you need?"

"What?"

He was pretty sure he noticed her cheeks flush at the question.

"Batteries. What size does your flashlight need?"

"Right. I have it written down," she said as she dug around in her purse. "Two, CR2032 sized batteries." She looked up at Jack. "What? You have a weird look on your face."

"It's just strange...I've never heard of a flashlight that takes disc batteries...must be some kind of fancy big-city type." He gave her a grin before turning around and looking through some small drawers.

"Yeah, something like that," Claire mumbled.

Jack handed her the batteries. He looked over the counter at her shoes. "I'm glad you're not in clogs, but those won't be any good either once the snow shows up." He motioned to her boots.

"These? These are Uggs...the warmest and most comfortable boot ever. Look, they've got a non-slip tread...I'm not going to fall down in these," she pointed to the soles with a smile on her face, "*and* they're made in Australia." She looked at him with a look of triumph.

"Yeah, I'm sure the Australians are big experts on snow." He chuckled. "Once you step into a deep drift, those boots are going to be filled with snow, not to mention that the suede won't hold up...they'll be ruined in no time." As soon as he'd said this, Jack felt bad. Her face had gone from triumphant to crestfallen. "I just would hate to see you ruin such a nice-looking pair of boots, that's all." He smiled gently at her.

"Thanks—"

"Oh, it's *you*." Hank had walked in from the back stockroom. He had his hands in his pockets as he rocked back on his feet. "Where's the Dodgers' cap?" he motioned to the top of Claire's head.

"I get it," she responded, pointing to Hank's cap. "You're a Boston fan, my condolences." She had a small, mischievous smile on her face.

"Your condolences? For what? We've won four World Series in the past twenty years...pffft...you're just sore that we beat you in '18." Hank was getting ready to go to the mat over his beloved Red Sox, when he suddenly looked at his phone. "Hey, Jenny just pulled some apple pies out of the oven," he said to Jack, his voice full of unconstrained excitement.

"Sorry—but you get texts when there's *pie?*" Claire looked at Hank with a look of disbelief on her face.

"Yeah...so what?" Hank replied.

Jack stepped in before this went any further. "Jenny makes the best apple pie you've ever tasted. They're gone in no time, so she gives us a heads-up when she's got them. As a matter of fact, how about joining me for a slice? She also makes a mean cup of coffee." Jack felt his heart hang in the balance as he waited for an answer.

"Sure, sounds good, I'm not a girl who says no to pie."

"Hey...what about me?" Hank said to Jack, his hands on his hips.

"I'll bring you back a slice," Jack said.

"Make it two," Hank replied as he gave Jack a thumbs up and a sly grin when Claire wasn't looking.

* * *

"OH MY GOD, this is so good." Claire had just taken a bite of the pie along with some of the vanilla ice cream. It really was the best pie she'd ever tasted.

"See? Now you don't think we're so weird getting a pie text." He smiled at Claire as he took a bite of his.

"Nah, I still think you guys are weird." She gave him a wink before taking another bite.

Jenny came over and refilled their coffee cups.

"What made you enlist in the army?" Claire asked. She noticed he seemed a bit uncomfortable with the question, his posture seemed to stiffen.

After a few seconds, he shrugged his shoulders. "The men in my family have always served. My dad was in Vietnam and my grandfather served in World War II, and my great-grandfather was in World War I. It's just what us Wilson men do. We feel a duty to give back." He remained quiet as he ran his fork along the crust of the pie.

"That's really amazing. How long were you there?"

"Six years, I enlisted right out of college."

A comfortable silence settled around them for a few minutes as they both enjoyed their pie and coffee.

Claire looked at him as he ate. She imagined he was thinking about Afghanistan. He seemed to be a million miles away. He had that handsome yet boyish quality some men had; his eyes could melt her core in less than a millisecond. "You mentioned you have a sister," she said, breaking the silence as she took a sip of her coffee.

"Beth, she's a couple of years older than I am. She and her husband are living in the house we grew up in."

"Is that going to make the holidays more difficult? You know...the memories...now that your dad isn't here?"

"Maybe, I hadn't thought about it that way."

"It's why I came out here. I didn't want to be reminded at every turn that my parents weren't around. I'm living in their house. It's hard. I don't want to be reminded all the time that they used to live there, yet I don't want to change it either." She took a deep breath as she took another bite of the pie.

"I get that," Jack said, looking her in the eye. "Beth actually remodeled the kitchen recently…I didn't think it was a good idea at first. It looks totally different, but I think it has actually helped. It's still the same house, but changed. It's how I feel about myself since serving and losing Dad: same guy but changed." His face softened, and he looked down at his mug.

Claire nodded as she listened to him.

"Dad always made Christmas special…magical, really. This was going to be our first Christmas together now that I'm home from Afghanistan, but…" Jack's voice trailed off.

"I'm so sorry Jack. I understand how hard it is." She reached out and put her hand on his wrist.

"Thanks…it's hard, she and her husband are expecting their first baby though, so that's brightened everyone's mood."

"Oh, that's exciting," replied Claire. "When's she due?"

"Around the end of January."

"So, she's pretty far along then. How's she doing?"

"Well, she was just ordered on bedrest…she has preeclampsia."

"Yikes…*total* bedrest?"

"Yep."

"That's going to make Christmas tough."

"We'll figure it out," Jack replied.

They sat quietly while finishing their coffee and pie. Claire stole glances at Jack at every opportunity. He was wearing his signature flannel shirt, biceps straining the fabric.

"Thank you for the pie," she said as they left the diner.

"Sure. I'm glad you enjoyed it." Jack was holding the bag containing Hank's two slices.

"Well, I guess I'll see you around," Claire said. She didn't really want to leave. She wished they were still inside eating pie. Being around him gave her a warm feeling inside.

"Yeah, see you around." Jack waved as he headed back to the store across the street.

Claire morosely made her way to her car. *At least I have the batteries.* She got in, turned the ignition on and…nothing. Turned it again and…nothing. "Is *everything* with a battery just going to crap out on me?" She hit her hands on the steering wheel before resting her forehead on it. *I do not need this right now.* She sat there for about a minute or two before she heard tapping on the passenger side window. *Jack!*

"Hi," she said brightly, getting out of the car.

"Are you having trouble? I saw you just sitting here and then when you began pounding on the steering wheel, I figured I better come check on you."

"That's so nice, thank you." Her cheeks were burning, and her heart was racing.

"Small town benefits."

"Thank you, I'm guessing it's the battery?" She shrugged her shoulders.

"Do you always have such bad luck with batteries?" He laughed lightly. "I've gotcha. Be right back."

In a minute he was back with his truck, pulling it forward until the front barely touched the front of Claire's car. To Claire it looked like the two cars were kissing. *What are you, eight years old? Get a grip, Claire.*

Jack jumped out and popped the hood, jumper cables in hand. In under five minutes, Claire's car was up and running again.

"Thank you," she said.

"No problem. Drive it around so the battery charges up.

You might still have an issue in the morning. If you do, just call me. If the battery's shot, you'll need to trade it in for a new rental."

He closed her door and waved as she drove off. Claire's heart was full of good feelings as she drove away. She drove for awhile out of town before figuring that she'd charged the battery enough and headed back home.

Her thoughts were on Jack during the entire drive back to the cottage. She didn't know him very well yet felt strangely drawn to him. She'd been hoping after the pie that he would have asked her out. *Is that really a good idea, though?* What was she thinking getting her mind wrapped up in this guy? I'm only going to be here for about a month and then back to Los Angeles, she thought. *What's the point?* Except for…which reminded her of the batteries.

First things first, she thought as she opened the cottage door. The house was super cold. A warm fire would be cozy and take the chill off, she thought. There was everything she needed right next to the fireplace: a small stack of newspapers, some kindling, logs, and long handled wooden matches. Claire built everything up the way her father had done when they had stayed in a cabin at Big Bear. Those were fun family trips. Claire had learned how to ski, albeit badly. They would ski during the day and then come back to the cozy cabin for dinner and games. Although at times, Claire wished she hadn't been an only child, the advantage had been that her parents' focus had been 100% on her. Their little family of three had been close. Claire's heart ached with loss. She refocused on getting the fire started.

Once the newspaper had caught, she headed back to the bedroom with the batteries in hand. She replaced the batteries and the vibrator roared to life with the flick of a switch. *Finally.* Claire was about to get comfortable when she heard the doorbell. *Shit.*

She left the bedroom and found the living room filled with smoke. *What the hell?* She flung the front door open with one hand while she went to see what was causing all the smoke, grabbing one of the pillows off the entry bench and waving it around in the air. When the door swung open, Jack was standing there with a package under one arm.

"Oh wow, what's going on in here?" He quickly set the package down and went to the fireplace. "Open the windows," he said to Claire. "And bring me an oven mitt or a towel from the kitchen."

Claire rushed the oven mitt to Jack as he kneeled in front of the fireplace. All the smoke was billowing into the room instead of up the chimney.

"You forgot to open the damper," he said as he used the mitt to push it open. Immediately, the room began to clear.

"Thank you. What good timing you have," she said.

"Yeah, I'm glad I was here." He returned the mitt to the kitchen and washed his hands.

"So, what brings you by?" Claire's heart was beating fast, and it wasn't from the fireplace mishap. Here he was in her living room; his tight jeans hugging his tall frame.

"I brought you something," he said, handing her the package. "Sorry, the wrapping isn't great."

"Looks fine," Claire said excitedly. *He brought me a gift... that's a good sign.* She smiled at Jack as she tore the paper from the box. She pulled the lid off and peered inside. "Oh, wow...boots." *Ugly boots.* She pulled them from the box, examining the heavy, black rubber soles. They were slightly taller than ankle height with big black laces. The only thing cute about them was the shearling lining. "Thanks?" She said, holding one of the boots out as she looked at it.

"I got your size when I retrieved your clog. I know, I know...they're not fashionable, and they're made in Maine, not Australia. They may not be the latest fashion by L.A.

standards, but here in River Falls once the snow arrives? You'll blend right in…and your feet will stay dry."

She thought she saw a slight blush on his cheeks. She may not love the boots, but the thought was pure sweetness.

"Thank you," she said. "I really appreciate you thinking about me." She held his gaze for a minute.

"You're welcome."

"And thank you again for giving me a jump today. I'm glad you were there."

"No problem. Really, almost anyone in town would have stopped to help."

"And thank you for preventing a house fire."

"It wouldn't have burned down…just smoke…but yeah, I'm glad I was here."

"I really owe you…big! I was about to make some hot chocolate…want some?"

"Sure, sounds good." He sat down on the sofa in the living room.

Claire looked out at him while she dumped two packets of the hot chocolate mix into mugs and added hot water. *Who cares if I'm only here for a month? I have needs and this might be just the person to fill those needs.*

CHAPTER 6

*J*ack was a bit disappointed at Claire's reaction to the boots. He got it…they weren't stylish for a big city girl, nevertheless, she'd looked like a kid on Christmas morning who didn't get what she'd asked Santa for. But she sure looked sexy as hell in her jeans and body-hugging sweater. Just seeing her made his heart beat faster.

Claire set a mug down next to him. "Here's my secret ingredient," she said, producing a small bottle of peppermint schnapps. She tipped a healthy portion into his mug.

"Thanks," Jack replied. He looked down at the small marshmallows floating around before fishing one out and tasting it. "These aren't the homemade ones you blogged about, or the French-style hot chocolate," he said trying to chew the small rubbery piece that had lodged itself into his molar as he eyed the watery drink.

"Uh…no…I haven't had a chance to make those yet, you'll have to make do with the instant kind with the marshmallows already included. It's all they had at the market," she said with a shrug of her shoulders. "I'm limited to what they have in stock…it's definitely not Los Angeles," she snorted.

"Right." He felt a little ruffled by her dig at the market. "Schnapps is an excellent addition though." Jack drank a bit more. Claire sat next to him on the couch, her shoulder touching his and now her leg had brushed against his leg. He felt his insides bolt to life. They continued to sit quietly with one another, enjoying the silence and the beauty of the fire. He was thinking all kinds of thoughts as he finished his drink. All of them were about the woman sitting next to him. The alcohol gave him the bit of liquid courage he needed. "So…I did *kind* of have something I wanted to ask you." He turned, facing Claire. His heart felt as if it had traveled up to his throat.

"Sure," she replied, her face brightened with what looked like expectation. "I owe you for the boots, not to mention rescuing my car today."

"I told you that my sister is pregnant and on bedrest…her husband, Tyler, isn't really the *handy* type, plus he travels a lot for work, so…she can't count on his help right now." He tried to clear the lump in his throat, but it wasn't budging. "Beth is *really* wanting a special Christmas since this will be our first one together in six years—and I told you how much Christmas meant to our dad."

He noticed what looked like apprehension slowly replace the expectation from her face.

"Well…I…I mean we were thinking that since you're an expert on these things, I was wondering, and Beth was wondering, whether you'd be willing to help us with Christmas." He looked her in the eyes…they were brown pools of warmth he wanted to dive into. "We would love to have you enjoy the holiday *with* us…unless, of course, you were planning on spending it alone…if so, I understand." His heart was about to beat out of his chest while he waited for her answer.

He wanted her to say yes, not for the Christmas stuff, but for his own selfish benefit…he wanted to spend time with her. A lot of time.

He thought he noticed her hesitate briefly before putting her hand on his arm and giving him a warm smile. "I'd love to help."

"That's awesome…thank you. Beth is going to be *so* happy; I have a long list from her of projects and recipes she'd gotten from your blog. I'll send it to you. Wow…what a relief. I won't have to tackle it alone."

"Long list? From the blog?" Claire responded…it seemed to Jack as if the color had suddenly drained from her face.

"Yeah…it's not *super* long. And we don't have to do *everything* on it either…we'll figure it out. You and I." He beamed as he looked at her. "I'll text you her address…maybe we could meet over there tomorrow…you'll like her, and she's going to be so excited to meet you. He noticed Claire wasn't saying anything…she'd gone mute after he'd mentioned the list. "I'll see you tomorrow…thank you again, Claire. This means the world to me." He looked into her eyes, which still seemed glazed over, said goodbye and got into his truck. *Maybe she's just tired.*

JACK PULLED INTO HIS DRIVEWAY. He'd had his head in the clouds the entire way after leaving Claire. She was so damn cute *and* sexy. He was a tiny bit concerned by the change in her once she'd agreed to help, but he chalked that up to her still adjusting to the time change. *Yeah, that's probably it.* The idea of spending time with her made him happy, and he needed something to feel happy about these days. Adjusting to civilian life after six years in Afghanistan had been a challenge. He'd just been getting a handle on the transition when his dad had died.

Jack was overwhelmed with feelings of grief and loss by the death of his father and the death of the young man under his charge. He was wracked with guilt over losing Robbie. He felt responsible. He awoke many nights covered in sweat... heart pounding and momentary confusion about where he was. He'd slowly remember that he was home in River Falls. The relief he felt was cut short once he remembered his dad was gone.

After he and Beth buried their father and got a grip on his financial affairs, Jack rolled up his sleeves and went to work trying to figure out where the store stood financially. He felt conflicted about rescuing the struggling business.

On one hand, it was his legacy...it had been passed down through generations; Jack felt an obligation to not let it falter on his watch. Even if he never settled down or had kids, Beth was having a son. He felt he owed it to his unborn nephew to not lose the store. He also felt an obligation to the town. While some did their shopping on Amazon or over at the Walmart, there were a lot of town folks who'd stayed loyal to the shop. It had been more of a community than a business. People would stop by for whatever they needed and talk to his dad, exchanging stories of trips, grandchildren, and town gossip. Some would say that Wilson's Hardware was the heart of the town...its life blood. How could Jack just let that disappear?

On the other hand, had been his desire to leave River Falls, to make a life in a bigger city. He'd left for Afghanistan with a broken heart. It had been rough, but the years had finally healed it; however, serving in a war zone hadn't given him any opportunity to meet someone new. He thought a life in Hartford would give him that chance. A big city, where you didn't know everyone. A fresh start. But that was becoming a distant hope. He needed to face facts: he was probably going to be living out his life here in River Falls.

And that's why these crazy feelings over a woman he barely knew were just that...*crazy.* She would be back in L.A. in a matter of weeks. Anything he started with Claire was going to wind up at one big dead end; what was the point? This realization didn't stop the tug his heart felt when he thought of her. The desire to spend more time with her, protect her...kiss her soft-looking lips and hold her in his arms and pull her tight. *Get her out of your head, Jack.* He opened his front door and let out a big sigh as he walked into the dark and lonely house.

* * *

"WHAT WERE YOU THINKING?" Emmy's voice was just a notch below a shriek. "I mean...you don't know how to do *any* of this...what are you going to do?"

"I don't know...I wasn't thinking with my head...I was thinking with something else." The enormity of what Claire had agreed to was beginning to sink in. *What was I thinking?* "I was thinking that I wanted to help him and his sister for Christmas. This is their first Christmas without their dad, I understand the sense of loss. I mean...I've got to be of *some* help? Right?" She looked expectantly at her friend.

"Okay...let's regroup." Emmy's voice had come down a few octaves. "We can handle this...I'll help you."

"But you're not *here.*" Claire said sadly.

"We'll do it by phone and Facetime...I'll help you through this. You've got this, Claire. We'll make a list of projects you can handle."

"There's already a list...but I can't handle *any* of it."

"What list?"

Claire told Emmy about the list Beth had already drawn

up. "I'll text it to you. But trust me…I can't do any of the things on it. Jack said he could handle a couple of them…but the rest? *Shit*."

"Send me the list…I'll see what I can do."

"Okay…thank you. Ugh…I'm so stupid, Emm."

"No, you're not…you're just horny." Emmy laughed and Claire couldn't help but join in.

"But it wasn't just that, Emm…I really want to help if I can. You always say that some of what you do should have stuck in my brain…maybe it has. I'm meeting Jack at his sister's house tomorrow…I'll let you know how it goes."

After hanging up, Claire poured another healthy shot of schnapps into her hot chocolate and pulled up the blog she'd written a couple of years ago.

Ooh La La!

While in Paris recently, I sampled my way through the French version of hot chocolate, and I have one word for it: luscious! There was nothing better than sitting outside a small cafe with my pot of le chocolate chaud and watching fashionable Parisians go about their day. The hot chocolate was unlike its American counterpart in that it was thick, rich, and velvety, practically as thick as a milk shake. I can assure you, though, you don't need to travel to Paris to enjoy this exquisite treat. The secret? Use the best ingredients and don't rush the process. Yes…I know…the skim milk hot chocolate you've been making is better for your figure…but trust me…this version is worth the extra thirty minutes on the treadmill…I promise! You will need to find high quality semi-sweet chocolate…when I say high quality, I mean something from Belgium or Switzerland. You will also need a high-quality whipping cream, brown sugar, and flaked fleur de sel. I went a step further and added homemade marshmallows to give it a bit of an American touch. Don't be intimidated. Homemade marshmallows are easy to whip up and only take a few quality ingredients. Once you try the homemade version, you'll have a hard time eating those chewy, flavorless store-bought ones. It's easier than you think to elevate your style of living. Click here for the full recipe. Au revoir!

CLAIRE HAD ALWAYS WRITTEN these blog posts to inspire people to live their best lives with creative recipes and crafts. She'd never thought twice about using a healthy dose of creative license, although Emmy sometimes tried to reign her back. But when reading them through Jack's eyes, through the perspective of him believing she could create *any* of this, all she could do was cringe inside. How am I going to live up to *this* version of myself? *I can barely live up to the real version of myself.* The thought worried her and gave her a sickening pit at the bottom of her stomach. *Ugh.*

CHAPTER 7

"*O*h my god, I can't believe it's *you!*" Beth pulled Claire in for a giant hug, "I'm Beth, but you know that already." Jack's sister had the same dark blond hair he did, except she had beautiful curls, the kind Claire had always dreamed of having. She had the same blue eyes as his and the most adorable dimples, and her energy was infectious.

"I'm glad to meet you, too," Claire said. She looked at Beth's pregnant belly. It was huge…like *really* huge. *She can't be just thirty-two weeks along.* "Are you having tw—" She noticed Jack's eyes practically bulge out of his head as he began to slightly, yet urgently, shake his head "no" while pulling an imaginary knife along his throat. "I mean…are you having a tough time with the bed rest?" She saw Jack heave out the breath he'd been holding in relief.

"You have *no* idea…all I want to be doing is decorating for Christmas. It feels like torture being confined all day to this," Beth replied, getting back into the quilt covered bed.

Claire heard a loud snort and noticed the Scottie dog lying underneath the covers. "Oh…cute, who's this?" she asked, scratching the dog on his head.

"That's Archie," Beth said. "He's under house arrest."

"House arrest?"

"He got the neighbor's dog pregnant."

At the sound of his name, Archie's head popped up. He made a "hmph" sound, jumped off the bed, and ambled out of the room; evidently not wanting to listen to the tale of his crime.

"Oh no," Claire replied, although it sounded kind of adorable.

"Oh *yeah*. He got under the fence one day while Pippa, our neighbor Sheila's Westie, was out. Archie must have been able to smell that she was in heat, because he dug a hole, that I swear he used a backhoe for, and was in their yard going at Pippa within seconds."

Claire had to stifle a giggle at the image Beth just painted.

"As luck would have it, just the one time did the trick. Pippa's due any day now." Beth had a look of pure exasperation on her face.

"You can't blame him," Jack piped up. "I mean…"

Beth shot Jack a look. "His punishment was a trip to the vet the very next week," she said. Jack appeared to visibly wince at this.

Claire couldn't help but let out a small laugh; evidently, this counted as trouble in a small town.

"Anyhoo…I had Tyler get down all the boxes of Dad's Christmas stuff. He put them in the sunroom. I thought you two could go through them and decide what to use…I think some ornaments are missing hooks. Claire, instead of all those ugly metal ones, you could replace them with some red satin ribbon. Wouldn't that look great?!?"

This sounded like a project Claire could tackle. "Great idea," she replied, giving Beth a thumbs up signal.

"Get some rest, Sis, Claire and I'll start with the boxes. Do you need anything?"

"No…I'm good. I'm just delighted that you're here, Claire." Beth's face beamed, her dimples flanking her smile.

* * *

JACK AND CLAIRE had been sorting through the boxes for a couple of hours. They'd created a box of things to be used and repackaged what wouldn't be. The time had flown by. She and Jack had exchanged small talk, little nuggets about one another. Claire learned Jack had been an Eagle Scout and that he was quite an accomplished carpenter. "Yet you decided to study business. Why?"

"I don't know…I guess I wanted out of River Falls and it seemed that a degree in business would lead me to a career out of here. Few businesses around here need someone with a business degree."

Claire nodded her head. She looked over at him as he slid one box back into the closet. His shirt had come untucked from his jeans and Claire could see part of a six-pack peeking out. Jack caught her staring at him. Luckily, she hadn't been drooling too, but she could feel her cheeks turn red.

"So how did you get into the blogging business?" Jack stopped what he was doing and looked at her.

"It started with a college project and it just kind of took off."

"That's amazing. You're so talented. I'm really in awe of all that you can do."

Claire felt a sense of discomfort. "Well…you know, like most blogs, I'm sure, a lot of creative license is used; I'm not really all that." She looked at Jack. Her heart was racing. How far was she going to go?

"What do you mean?" He stopped what he was doing.

"Well…" She felt tongue tied. "Everything is staged in the photos and…"

Beth suddenly burst into the room; her face appeared ready to burst with excitement. "I just got off the phone with Sheila. I'd told her all about you; she scrolled through your blog posts and came across the one where you built a whelping box and helped birth a litter of puppies! Remember? You'd even nursed one back to life! It was just the sweetest story." Beth gushed with excitement.

Claire began to get a queasy feeling in her stomach. She remembered the post. It had been one of her more *creative* ones. She remembered Emmy standing, arms folded, giving Claire one of *those* looks. At the time, Claire thought it was just a little creative embellishment…but now…but *now*…oh god…she felt as if she was going to be ill at the thought of what was coming next.

"Neither Sheila, nor I have *any* experience birthing puppies. It would be crazy good if you could build Pippa an adorable whelping box to welcome her puppies in!" Claire was sure Beth was about to combust with excitement.

"Well…I…uh…I'm probably going to have my hands full with your Christmas list." She looked over at Jack.

"It wouldn't be that hard…I can do the actual building if that would help. It sure would be cute for Pippa to have a *real* whelping box instead of the cardboard one Sheila's got set up now." He smiled confidently at Claire. "We've got this."

"We do?" she asked quietly.

"Sure," Jack replied, hands on his hips.

"Okay," was all she could manage to croak out. Her throat was suddenly as dry as the Sahara.

"Also…it would be really great if you could assist with the birth." Beth was bubbling over now with delight. "Because Sheila doesn't know what she's doing, and I obviously can't help." Beth motioned to her enormous belly.

Just then, Archie had sidled up to Jack and looked around at everyone, somehow knowing the conversation had something to do with his little escapade. He let out a sharp bark that startled everyone.

"Okay...I'll see what I can do." Claire felt clammy and weak in the knees. She could check out some online videos...see how it's done. *How hard could it be?* Animals gave birth out in the wild all the time without *any* help. She'd probably just need to give Pippa some emotional support, like a doggie doula. *Pippa* would do all the work. Claire felt a moment of relief. But the fact remained that she was horribly squeamish at even the *thought* of blood. A career in medicine had never and would never enter her mind.

"Great! It's all settled then. I'll go call Sheila, you could pop over now and meet Pippa to get an idea of what size box you'll need to build." Beth was hurriedly walking back to her bedroom.

"Let's walk over, I'll introduce you to Sheila." Jack held the front door open. Archie trotted out ahead of him, he seemed to know where they were headed.

"Hi! I'm Sheila, come on in." The curvy blond stepped aside so that Jack and Claire could step into the house. Archie had slipped in past their feet and pranced off.

"Let's follow his lead...he always knows where Pippa is," Sheila said.

The little black Scottie trotted into the family room and up to a blue and white striped dog bed where he nuzzled the small white dog lying there.

"This is Pippa," Sheila announced proudly. "She's due any day...she and Archie had a one-night stand, I guess you could call it." She gave Archie a disapproving look.

Claire kneeled and gave the little Westie a scratch on her head. Pippa's belly was large, and she looked miserable over the entire ordeal. "You should have used protection," Claire whispered. Archie let out a snort.

"I have a tape measure here, if you want to take down some measurements." Sheila held it out. Claire had no idea what to measure.

Jack took the tape measurer from Sheila. "Where are you going to be putting it?" he asked.

"Here in the family room. That way she's with all of us, and not hidden away somewhere. I looked over your blog and that box you built was so adorable! Since it *will* be the focal point of the room, I really want it to blend in, like a piece of furniture. Did Beth tell you about Pippa's Instagram account?"

Claire shook her head no. *The dog is on social media?*

"She's got over ten thousand followers! I'm going to be posting photos and videos of the whole thing. Having a beautiful whelping box will help make it go viral."

CLAIRE DUMPED a handful of ice into the glass and poured a healthy portion of bourbon over it. She needed it after the day she'd had. *Whelping box? Birthing puppies?* She felt as if she was going to cry. Thank goodness Jack took over the building of the box. He seemed to know what he was doing… mentioned something about trimming it in decorative crown molding. When the discussion had turned to the idea that Claire could *sew* the bedding, she'd let out a strangled little laugh. She had no idea what end was up on a sewing machine. Claire had been quick on her feet and noted that time was of the essence, and it would be too challenging to sew the bedding from scratch and instead introduced the idea of using a gently used quilt to pad the box. She had stopped by the secondhand shop on the way back to the cottage and had hit the jackpot. They had a lovely, blue and white floral-patterned quilt…it would look great. Claire was pretty sure she could sell the idea to Sheila.

But now the birthing. What in the actual hell was she going to do? She took a large swallow of the bourbon and sat down with her laptop. It was time to face the music and remind herself exactly what she had written. The rest of the bourbon went down the hatch before Claire focused her eyes on the computer screen.

PUPPY LOVE

This weekend I had the very special honor of helping bring six tiny pups into the world. It was an experience I'll never forget! But let's back up a bit and talk about what you'll need to help your dog have her special day. Dogs give birth in what is called a "whelping box." This is a type of enclosure with sides tall enough that the new little nuggets can't escape. The whelping box is where momma dog will give birth and then nurse and tend to her puppies until they're old enough to expand their horizons. Now, most whelping boxes are plywood, or PVC tubing, cardboard, or even an old dresser drawer, and then they're often filled with rags or old bath towels. However, there is no reason you can't make a more beautiful place for your dog to birth and nurture her little darlings.

I painted the one I made for Snickers' litter white on the outside (with non-toxic paint…those pups will chew everything once their teeth come in!). I added crown molding trim to really elevate the look. I found the most beautiful blue and white ticked fabric that I turned into the most adorable and luxurious mini duvet, which I layered over an orthopedic dog bed, topped with a soft lambswool mattress pad (cut to size), of course this was all covered in water-proof sheeting, and then the beautiful duvet topped it all off. Snickers was truly a queen for a day!

And when that day came, it was a miracle. Watching Snickers give birth to her puppies was truly amazing...nature at its best. We did our best to keep momma calm and comfortable while we aided the birth. As soon as the puppies arrived, we cleaned them up and then nudged them to nurse. I noticed one puppy had stopped breathing. I rolled him on his back while in the palm of my hand and gently, but firmly, stroked from the head down to the tail on both sides. After a few seconds, he began to breathe. I'm so grateful for this because losing him would have been a sad note to an otherwise beautiful experience. Oh...and don't forget to identify the puppies by tying different color pieces of satin ribbon around their necks so that you can keep track of each pup. I've attached pictures from this very special day. FYI, little Jasper is doing just fine. He's gaining weight and can hold his own with his littermates. A truly beautiful experience. I was grateful I could take part in Snicker's special day.

Follow the link below for step-by-step instructions for building the whelping box, and for the construction of the bedding. Hugs to the new momma.

CLAIRE SAT in stunned silence after she'd finished reading the post. Her aggressive creativity was going to bite her in the you know what. She poured a bit more bourbon into her glass and sat back on the couch, a small fire keeping the room warm; she'd better watch some videos and prepare for puppy midwifery. Claire let out an enormous sigh and closed her eyes. *It'll be okay, Claire. You've got this!* But she didn't have it. She dreaded what was facing her.

She called Emmy and told her the whole story. Emmy had laughed so hard she couldn't stop. Claire could actually hear tears in her eyes...she laughed that hard. Claire had gotten moody about it and had said goodbye and hung up. Maybe it *was* funny. She sure wished she felt like laughing instead of how she really felt, like sobbing.

At least she was spending time with Jack. The more time she spent with him, the more she liked him. He was solid in a quiet way. He was thoughtful, kind, funny, and sexy as hell. Her core felt like red hot lava when she was near him…him and his damn sexy flannel shirts. She was yearning for something more…*anything* more from him.

CHAPTER 8

$\mathcal{O}$ ver the next few days, Jack and Claire worked side by side, going through all the boxes of Christmas things. They'd sorted out what they could use and re-boxed the remaining items. Claire was proud of herself; she'd replaced all the metal hooks on the ornaments with loops of red satin ribbon. It looked good and Beth had loved it.

"Okay…I think we're ready to get the trees." Jack looked at Claire with a twinkle in his eyes. "It's a bit of a drive, so we should get going."

"Sure, let me grab my things."

They climbed into Jack's truck, first stopping at Jenny's grabbing two black coffees to go. Claire felt thrilled to be spending time alone with Jack; the past few days they'd spent quite a bit of time together. She enjoyed being with him. He possessed a quality she couldn't quite put her finger on. It was something that made her feel comfortable and safe. She glanced over as he was driving. He looked sure of himself, confident. But where was all this leading to? There was no end game that ended in a relationship, at least not from Claire's vantage point. In a few weeks, she would be back in

LA and Jack would be here. He looked over at her and smiled.

A few minutes passed in silence.

"What are you thinking about?" he asked.

"Me? Oh, I was just thinking about Christmases past." She felt a swell of emotions as she thought about her parents. She missed them a lot.

He took one hand off the wheel and covered Claire's hand. Just that one little gesture made her feel better. She wasn't sure exactly why, but it did.

"Did you usually cut your trees down? I mean, I know from your blog that you do now, but what about when you were a kid?"

"Uh...no, we didn't. For a few years we had an artificial tree." She looked over at Jack and thought she saw a look of horror momentarily wash over his face. "It was easy. It opened like an umbrella. All we had to do was plug it in. My mom claimed it let off something toxic that was causing her headaches, so my dad eventually ditched it. After that, we usually picked one up at Vons."

"Vons? What's that? A tree lot?" He glanced over at her.

"It's a supermarket."

"A *supermarket*? You got your Christmas tree at a *supermarket*? I'm not sure which is worse...that...or the fake one."

Claire made a face at him. "Well, not everyone lives out in the middle of nothing where you can just go cut one down." She motioned to the many pine trees they were passing.

"But you're able to do that now...so it *is* doable, even if you live in L.A."

Claire and Emmy had done this exactly *once* for the blog and it had been a major pain in the ass. The drive to the tree farm took nearly two hours, it had been hot walking around looking for the perfect tree and then they'd driven no faster than 40 miles per hour on the freeway all the way back, worrying that the tree was going to snap from the top of Claire's Honda. Angry L.A. drivers were roaring past them, leaning on their horns; some even giving them a middle finger salute.

Claire fidgeted in her seat. "Yeah—it's doable."

* * *

"Here, you're going to need these," Jack said. He handed Claire a pair of work gloves.

"What do I need these for?" she asked, turning the gloves over in her hands.

"The trees are sticky and sharp...*don't* you wear gloves when you get your own trees?" He looked at her quizzically.

"Well, yeah, but *they* did the actual cutting...not us...we're girls." She gave him a tentative smile and a shrug of her shoulders.

"Don't tell me girls can't cut a tree down, you just didn't *want* to cut it down." He laughed as he walked off. Claire followed hurriedly after him.

"The point was to get a fresh tree...not to get a lumberjack workout in," she snorted, following him as he walked through the tree farm. Dark green trees dotted the land for as far as you could see.

Whenever he could, Jack took in the vision of Claire. She looked sexy in her figure-hugging jeans and pink flannel shirt. And she was wearing the boots he'd gotten her.

"How are you liking those?" He nodded towards her feet.

"They actually feel okay, thank you again, it was really sweet of you to think of me and my footwear." She smiled at him; her big brown eyes looked inviting.

"I'm happy to help. But remember, once the snow comes, you'll want to tuck your pants inside them to keep dry." At the mere mention of her pants, Jack imagined pulling those pants off her. *Get your head out of the clouds, Jack.* This…whatever *this* was, is going nowhere other than her going back to L.A.

"Okay…how about this one…looks pretty good, right?" He was standing by a beautiful 7-foot tree. "Does she look straight?" he asked.

Claire walked around the tree. "Yeah…looks good…I think you found a keeper."

"Great. Okay, I'll need you to hold on to the tree while I cut." He kneeled on the ground and sawed at the base of the tree.

"So…are you spending the holidays with anyone special?" Claire asked him.

Jack looked up from what he was doing. He couldn't see Claire's face, since it was obscured by the tree. "Special? Like my family?" But he knew exactly what she was asking. He just wanted to hear her say it.

"No—you know…*special* special."

Jack smiled. "You mean do I have a girlfriend." He said it as a statement, not a question.

She didn't respond.

Jack let a few seconds pass before answering. "No, I'm not spending it with anyone *special* special," he replied. He resumed sawing. "Remember the part where I told you it's hard to meet anyone in a small town?"

"But you haven't *always* been in a small town…what about college? What about during breaks from your tours in Afghanistan?"

Jack was quiet for a moment. He pulled the felled tree to the pathway and began to trudge further along. "We need to find two more."

"You're not answering my question."

He wasn't sure he wanted to answer. It had been a long time ago. What good was it to dredge it up? He stopped in front of a tree and looked over at Claire. "How's this one look?"

Claire gave him a thumbs up and braced the tree while he began to cut.

"Well?"

"There *was* someone…in college…Tara." He stopped sawing…looking up towards Claire.

"What happened?" she asked.

"We'd been together for two years, when she found out I was planning to enlist, she decided she didn't want any part of army life." Jack still felt a small tug on his heart at the memory. He'd loved her…a lot. It had crushed him when she'd given him the ultimatum: the army or her. He'd learned something about her that day that he hadn't previously known, and it was something that proved to be fatal to the relationship.

"Why?"

"You'd have to ask her. But I guess she had dreams of me being a big-time business exec and us living the good life in Boston or New York City, not on an army base. The thought of army life just wasn't appealing to her."

"Wow. I'm sorry, Jack. That was kinda shallow of her."

"Maybe," was all he said. He stood up and let the tree fall to the ground, coming face to face with Claire. There was a kindness in her eyes.

"Thank you for your service," she said. "I'm always amazed and thankful for the selfless-ness it takes to serve. You put your life aside…and risked it… to serve your country. It's honorable. She was a fool."

Jack just nodded his head. Claire's response warmed him. It had been the reaction he'd wanted from Tara. He brushed the dust from his gloves before looking up at her. "Okay, just one more."

"One more? Is Beth putting up *three* trees now? Oh my god she's gone crazy."

"Nope," Jack said, and then smiled. "One's for you. You deserve to have some Christmas spirit at the cottage." He continued to look at her, he felt a strong desire to embrace her. He imagined just how good that would feel.

"Thank you, that would be nice," she replied. Jack noticed a small blush come across her face.

They soon found a tree for Claire. Once again, she held firmly on to the tree while Jack sawed.

"So, what about you?" he said.

"What about me what?"

"Anyone *special* special waiting for you back in L.A.?" He momentarily stopped what he was doing while he waited for her response.

"Not anymore. We broke up about six months ago." Her voice was soft.

"What happened?" Jack resumed sawing. *She's single.*

"He couldn't understand why I was so depressed over my parents. He didn't understand. Kept telling me to *get over it.* He really flipped out when he'd heard I was seeing what he called *a shrink.*"

Jack stood up and let the tree fall to the ground, once again coming face to face with Claire. He wanted just then to scoop her up into his arms and tell her it was okay to not get over it. He wanted to tell her she deserved love and support, even if she *never* got over it. He gave her a nod of understanding and quietly held her hand as they walked back to the truck.

The ride home was quiet. Jack was thinking about what to do. He wanted to ask Claire out, but to what end? She was headed back to L.A. in just a few weeks…what was the point? But on the other hand, he wanted…no he *needed* to see more of her. *Just do it.*

He pulled up in front of Claire's place and pulled her tree from the back of the truck, along with a bucket. "I'm going to slice a bit from the bottom and place it in water. Let it sit overnight before bringing it in."

"Okay…I don't have any lights…or a stand, or even ornaments." She was biting her bottom lip. She looked sexy as hell.

"I'll grab some stuff from the store…we've got everything you'll need." He looked into her eyes. "I was wondering— whether I could take you out to dinner?"

She stopped chewing on her lip…a bit of color flushed over her face. "You mean like a date?"

"Yeah, like a date. There's a great Italian restaurant nearby. I think you'd like it." His heart pounded loudly as he waited for her reply.

"Sounds good," she said, a small smile on her face.

"Great. Tomorrow night around 7?" Jack felt a soar of happiness go through him.

She nodded her head. "Perfect."

* * *

JACK'S INSIDES melted a bit when he saw Claire open the door. She looked sexy in slim black pants and a fuchsia cashmere sweater with a low neckline.

"Hi," she said. "Come on in, I'm almost ready."

Jack walked into the cottage and took a seat on the couch while he waited for her. Inside he felt nervous but wasn't sure why. Sure, he'd been on many dates in the past, but had never felt as tingly and anxious as he did right now. He had been looking forward to this night since the second Claire agreed to go. He wasn't sure where any of this would lead to, but for now, he was just going to allow it to happen.

"Okay, ready," Claire said brightly.

She'd added some jewelry and a bit of lipstick. It made her lips look even more inviting. Jack cleared his throat and stood up. "You look beautiful." He helped her with her coat and opened the front door.

"Thank you." She beamed at him. "You don't look so bad yourself. I think this might be the first time I've seen you without a flannel shirt on."

Jack chuckled, holding the truck's door open while she stepped in. "Just trying not to be predictable." He closed the door and got in on the driver's side next to her. Her fragrance had filled the truck with the soft scent of vanilla and citrus. "You smell good," he said, turning the key and starting the engine. He smiled at Claire and noticed her blush in response.

"Thanks."

The restaurant was a twenty-minute drive to the next town. La Fattoria was in a small red farmhouse. Inside, the interior was homey yet elegant. A stone fireplace in the corner had a nice blaze going. Tablecloth covered tables were lit with flickering votive candles at their centers.

"This is adorable, and it smells so good," Claire said. She gave Jack a big smile. They sat in a quiet corner. The restaurant was lightly filled with other patrons.

"Their food is fantastic. It's all fresh and locally sourced," Jack said.

After placing their orders, they enjoyed some wine.

"To you, for agreeing to help me with Christmas," Jack said. He held his glass up to hers.

"You are so welcome. I just hope you're not disappointed," Claire responded before taking a sip.

"How could I be disappointed? This is what you do and you're great at it." He saw something flash across her face but couldn't decipher it. She'd mumbled something in response, but the server arrived just then, setting down a plate of mozzarella, drizzled with olive oil and served with warm focaccia.

"Oh my god that looks amazing," Claire said as she spread some of the cheese onto a piece of the bread. She closed her eyes as she took a bite. "It's *so* good." She opened her eyes and looked at Jack. They sat quietly as they consumed the tasty appetizer.

Jack leaned back in his seat and looked at Claire. Her dark brown eyes looked back at him.

"What do you like to do when you're not working?" he asked.

Claire was quiet for a moment before replying. "I love going to a Dodgers' game whenever I can. Nothing better than a hot dog, an ice-cold beer, and a baseball game…especially *Dodgers'* baseball." She smiled at him.

No Dodgers around here unless they're playing Boston.

"I also love to get in some golf whenever possible. I rarely have an entire day to play 18 holes, I mostly play just nine. There's a good pitch 'n putt course near me. My dad taught me how to play, it was something we did together."

No golf here six months out of the year, because of cold weather.

She continued. "I also love going to the beach. My house is within walking distance…I love going early in the morning to walk on the sand before many people are out. I also like to ride my bike along the path that borders the beach."

No beach here. It became crystal clear to Jack that all the things Claire loved to do mostly weren't doable in River Falls. He took a sip of his wine. He was a bit surprised she hadn't included cooking or crafting on her list, but maybe she considered that all work, he thought.

The server walked up with their entrees and set them down on the table. Lasagna with mushrooms, sausage, and ricotta cheese for Jack, and a ribbon pasta topped with pancetta in a tomato cream sauce for Claire.

"This looks fantastic," Claire said as she wound some pasta onto her fork. "Oh my god, and it *tastes* amazing," she said, closing her eyes as she chewed.

"I told you it was good."

"So, you know about me now. What do you like to do with *your* free time?" Claire asked him, a soft smile on her face.

"Me? I also like to go to baseball games. I try to go to Boston to watch the Sox a few times a year. There are also a few minor league teams within driving distance; those games are fun to go to."

"Not the Red Sox again." Claire made a fake groan as she gave him a teasing wink. "That guy, Hank, is super serious about the Sox."

"He is," Jack said and then chuckled. "If I ever so much as say one negative thing he'll blast me...and *I'm* a Sox fan, he's so not happy to hear *anyone* trash talk them."

"I'll be sure to keep that in mind," Claire said, a twinkle in her eye.

He took another bite of his food before continuing. "I also like to build things...lately I've been making birdhouses. I built that one at the cottage."

"The little yellow and white one?"

Jack nodded his head as he chewed. He noticed her face light up.

"It's adorable! Have you made others?"

"Yeah, I've had a few for sale at the store, they sell pretty quickly."

"You should totally build more and put them on Etsy... I'm serious."

"Maybe," Jack replied.

"Anything else you like to do?" she asked. Her eyes filled with curiosity.

"I like to read."

Claire nodded as she continued to eat. "Like what?"

"Oh…I don't know…most anything, except romance." He made a face.

"Hey…no judging romance readers. And besides, I don't think you're their demographic," she said with a smirk.

"Probably not," he replied. "Are you?" He smiled up at her.

"Well…" She began to chew on her bottom lip. Jack found it to be completely adorable.

She cleared her throat. "I didn't always appreciate romance books. I used to think they were just fluff."

"And now you don't?"

"Nope. I like the message of hope and love conquering all."

"And the sex." Jack smiled slyly at her.

"Well, yeah…there's that." Claire's cheeks were turning red. She cleared her throat before continuing. "I started reading to someone…Ruthie Blum at our local retirement home. I started reading to her when I was in high school. I've been reading to her at least once a week for over eleven years now."

"Let me guess, Ruthie likes romance novels." Jack smiled.

Claire's face brightened. "She does."

He loved how much her face came alive while telling him this.

"At first the books were the typical, bodice-ripping, historical romances…they were steamy but fairly tame. And then a few years ago she began to follow a couple of new authors that write romantic comedies. But the sex…oh my god! Some of them are practically x-rated!"

Jack laughed out loud. "What's Ruthie's reaction when you read those parts?"

"She usually will say 'oh my' or 'can you imagine?'"

Jack leveled his eyes at her. "Well? Can you imagine?" He watched as her face went from light red to crimson. He smiled.

"Don't try to embarrass me, Jack." She smiled before taking a sip of wine. "But I do have a funny story to tell. Ruthie used to listen to audio romances while in the common rec room. While it was the tamer bodice rippers no one minded. A few of the other residents would even listen with her. But one day she decided to start one of her new romcoms...well...when the other residents first heard the words c-o-c-k and p-u-s-s-y they were horrified. Ruthie was banned from playing anymore of her books in the rec room."

Jack laughed hard as he imagined this happening. He found it adorable that Claire couldn't say the words aloud, but instead spelled them out. "I really wish I could have seen their faces." He was still chuckling.

"I know. Me too actually." Claire giggled.

"Do you still read to Ruthie?"

"I do. I actually began go more often after I loss my parents. I love Ruthie, she's been a good person to talk to. So, it's been a two-way street for both her and I. Her niece is reading to her while I'm gone. She's got tons of extended family, so I don't worry too much about her."

They continued to talk as they finished their meal. Jack really liked the person he was getting to know. He was already thinking ahead to when they got back to her place. *But where am I going with this?*

They split a dessert of tiramisu and some coffees before making their way back to Claire's. Jack's heart was racing, and he felt a lump in his throat. He reached over and took Claire's hand in his as he drove. It was warm and soft. She gave his hand a little squeeze in response. Jack's core jolted in response, and he drove just a bit faster.

CHAPTER 9

They were back at Claire's; she'd invited Jack to come inside for a nightcap.

"I'm just going to get comfortable," Claire called out as she headed down the hall.

"Sure, I'll get a fire started," Jack responded.

"Perfect," she said, before disappearing into her room.

What are you doing, Claire? There's no road to a relationship here, she told herself. But her body wanted *more*. A lot more. Jack looked so sexy tonight. His V-neck sweater over a t-shirt and corduroy pants looked good on him. She took off her shoes and replaced them with some fuzzy socks. She switched out of her sweater and pulled on a sexy silk t-shirt. As she checked her face in the mirror, she fluffed up her hair with her fingers. *Here goes nothing.*

"Hey," Claire said, entering the room.

Jack was tending to the fire that was roaring pretty good. He'd removed his sweater and his well-muscled arms were displayed nicely in a t-shirt. He looked over at her and smiled, replacing the fire-poker in its stand before taking a seat next to her on the couch.

"This is nice," he said as he leaned back.

"It is," she replied, not sure where this was all leading, but hoping it was leading to something nice. "How about some hot chocolate?" She thought she saw a small look of discomfort come across his face.

"Got anything else?"

"Bourbon."

"Sounds good, on the rocks if you have 'em."

"Sure do," she said. "Be right back." In the kitchen, she poured two bourbons over ice and returned to sit next to Jack on the couch. It felt good to be close to him. He smelled good...clean mixed with that guy scent. This time, it was Claire who proffered the toast. "To new beginnings," she said, and clicked her glass against his before taking a sip. The smoky bourbon warmed her insides as it went down.

Jack put his arm around her, his hand on her shoulder. She was glad she'd removed the warm sweater; between the fire and Jack touching her, she was overheating...fast. He began to rub her shoulder lightly as they sat quietly, nursing their drinks. Claire closed her eyes as her body responded quickly to his touch.

She opened them and looked at Jack. It only took a second before he brought his hand to her chin and gently placed his lips on hers. At first the kiss was feathery soft and gentle like a whisper, but it slowly built up, becoming more intense, almost urgent. Her insides were melting quickly. She slowly slipped her tongue into his mouth; she heard him groan. He pulled back and looked at her, his blue eyes tender and warm; he drew her in again, kissing her passionately, his tongue now finding hers. Jack gently ran his hands through her hair, stroking her softly as his mouth kissed hers.

Claire let out a soft sound when his hands ran over the outside of her top, along the sides of her breasts. He trailed a finger across them, to her nipples, which even through her clothing were rock hard. He slowly drew circles around the erect nipples with his finger, causing Claire's desire to go from zero to sixty in a heartbeat. His hand drifted down the front of her and then rested on her leg before moving to the inner portion of her thigh. He ran his fingers over the material of her pants, stopping when they got to where her panties began.

Claire was going mad with desire. She softly ran her hands through Jack's hair, pulling him in close while they kissed. She felt his hands gently tug her shirt from her pants, soon touching her bare skin underneath. It felt as if her heart would burst with need. He stopped kissing her and looked her in the eyes as he slowly pulled her shirt off over her head. He then unhooked her bra, finally freeing her breasts. His hands soon found them, gently cupping each one before bringing his mouth to a nipple, softly flicking it with his tongue as he sucked. Claire was now moaning loudly, clutching his hair with her hands.

She brought his face up to hers, kissing him while running her hands over his body. She stood up in front of Jack, letting him undo the button of her pants and then slowly unzip them, all the while holding her gaze with his sexy eyes.

"Do you want me to continue?" he asked, his voice low and husky.

All Claire could do was nod in assent, her throat too dry to speak.

Jack pulled her pants down, allowing Claire to step out of them. He pulled her hips, which were level with his mouth, closer to him and ran his hands along the silky front of her dark blue panties, slowly sliding a finger just on the inside of them. He looked up at her as he found her most sensitive area. His fingers began to explore, slowly working through her folds. Claire's head tipped back. She gripped his shoulders with her hands while Jack gently pulled her panties off. She looked down at him as he stared at her naked body.

"You're beautiful, Claire. Simply beautiful." He ran his hands along the curve of her hips, brushing gently against her center. He stood up and pulled his shirt off, revealing a toned and sexy body.

She let out a small whimper at the sight of him and wrapped herself inside his arms as they continued to kiss, running her hands over his broad shoulders. *It's been too long.* She nibbled and kissed his neck, inhaling his scent. She soon moved to his ear, running her tongue along its lobe, gently sucking on it. "Maybe we should go to the bedroom," she whispered.

At that exact moment, Jack's phone buzzed. He quickly glanced at the screen.

"Shit, it's Beth—Tyler's out of town, I have to take this—it could be an emergency." He put the phone to his ear. "Beth… is everything okay? What? *Now*? Okay, we'll be right over… I'll bring Claire, she's here with me."

"What's going on?" Claire asked, her body melting to feel him against her.

"Pippa's in labor…we gotta go."

"What?!? Now?!?" *Shit!* "Great timing, Pippa," Claire grumbled under her breath as she grudgingly got dressed. Her body was not complying with the new agenda; she was completely hot and bothered and did not want to be putting clothing back *on*. She hadn't had sex in over six months and her entire being had been looking forward to a happy release with Jack. Instead, she would be helping Pippa push out puppies. Even Pippa had gotten some more recently than Claire. *Fucking dog.*

* * *

"HOW'S SHE DOING?" Jack asked Sheila. He and Claire had rushed over as soon as Beth had called. He kneeled next to the whelping box, stroking Pippa softly on the head.

"She seems okay. She passed the sac about 30 minutes ago. According to Dr. Sheehan, the first puppy should arrive within the hour...if not we need to get Pippa right over to her. Here, you'll need these," Sheila said.

Claire took the plastic bag of supplies from Sheila's hands and looked through it. "What's the dental floss for?" she asked, her brows knitted down. *We're not cleaning the dog's teeth, are we?*

"I thought you would know," Sheila said; a look of worry covered her face.

"I uh...didn't use floss with Snickers," she replied. *Shit, I don't remember reading about floss when I Googled this whole thing.* Panic gripped Claire's chest and throat. *I'm in way over my head.* She looked over at Pippa, who was giving her a side eye glance. *Even the dog knows I'm a fraud.*

"What did you tie off the umbilical cords with?" Sheila's voice was climbing a few octaves.

The umbilical cords? Claire felt clammy and nauseas. "We... uh...we just used some thread." The back of her neck prickled with sweat. "What are the scissors for?" Claire was afraid to ask. She was hoping they were to cut the floss with.

"It was on Dr. Sheehan's list...she said we'll need to use them if Pippa doesn't chew through the cords."

Oh my god! Please chew through the cords, Pippa. She looked over at Jack, who was giving her a quizzical look.

"Oh look! Here comes a puppy!" Sheila's shriek cut through Claire's foggy haze.

Claire's gaze went from Pippa's face to her bottom half, and she saw, to her horror, the head of a puppy pushing out...a slimy covering over it along with some pink tinged liquid oozing out. It was the last thing Claire remembered.

* * *

"WHAT'S HAPPENING?" Claire tried to sit up but felt woozy. Jack's face appeared in her sight.

"You passed out." He placed a bag of ice on one side of her forehead. "You hit the corner of the whelping box; you're going to have a nice size goose egg. Hopefully you don't have a concussion."

Claire reached up to the bag of ice, cradling it to her head. "How's Pippa?"

"She's on her second puppy. Everything's going okay. I looked over the instructions from the vet and can help Sheila with everything. You just stay lying down." He gave her a kiss on the forehead before returning to the whelping box.

"It's a girl!" Sheila cried out. "Oh Pippa, I'm so proud of you," she gushed. "Jack, let me get a pic while you cut the cord."

Claire felt like she was going to be sick at just the mention of the cord being cut. Good idea to just stay lying down, she thought. She closed her eyes and soon nodded off.

She woke to Jack softly calling her name. "I want to make sure you don't have a concussion," he said as he looked at her.

"I'm sure I'm fine," she replied. "But my head sure does hurt." She tentatively rubbed her hand along the lump that had formed.

"Let me get you some aspirin," Jack said. "I'll be right back."

"How's Pippa?" Claire croaked out.

"She's doing great," Sheila responded. "She had three puppies, two girls and one boy." Claire could hear the pride in her voice.

"That's good," Claire said. Jack handed her some aspirin and a glass of water. He helped her sit up so she could take it.

"I'm going to stay with you tonight...you need to be woken up every few hours to be sure you're not concussed."

"I don't think that's necessary," Claire said, but her insides warmed at the idea.

"It's that or I'm taking you to the hospital to be checked out."

She smiled up at Jack, the memory of his touch still fresh in her mind. "In that case, I'll take door number one," she said before laying her head back down.

* * *

CLAIRE CLIMBED INTO BED. She'd changed into her pajamas before letting Jack into the bedroom. "Where are you going to sleep?" she asked, her eyebrows raised slightly as she pulled the covers up around her waist.

"In the guest room," he replied, nudging his head towards the hall. "I'll come wake you up every three hours...just to be sure you're okay." He crossed his arms as he leaned against the door jamb.

"You *could* sleep in here," Claire said. She would love to have his gorgeous body next to hers, even if they would not be having sex.

"Put all of that on hold...I won't be able to help myself if I'm lying next to your beautiful and sexy body." He came over to the bed and brushed the hair from her forehead. "It would be torture not to touch you...I want to wait. If you're feeling better tomorrow, we can pick up where we left off."

Claire nodded her head. Her entire core had lit up at the thought of his hands on her body. "Okay," she squeaked out. She scooted down into the bed, her head on the pillow, the quilt pulled up to her chin.

Jack leaned down and kissed her on the lips. "Good night.

I'll see you in a few hours." He snapped off the light and left the door half open.

She could hear him close the door to the guest room. Because of a dog, she had a lump on her head and was going to bed sexually frustrated. "Thanks, Pippa," she grumbled as she tried to sleep.

CHAPTER 10

*C*laire awoke the next morning to the smell of coffee and bacon. She slipped into a robe and walked to the kitchen. Jack was in a white t-shirt and jeans, his back to her, cooking eggs. "Good morning," she said as she walked towards him.

"Hey, good morning. How do you feel?"

"I feel okay...a bit of a headache," she said, gingerly touching the knot on her head. Thank you for staying last night...I really appreciate it...and...you certainly didn't have to cook me breakfast."

"No need to thank me, I wanted to. It was my pleasure to stay here...I wouldn't leave you alone." He turned the stove off, turned and embraced her. His muscular arms around her felt like heaven first thing in the morning. She buried her nose into his chest...he smelled good, not like cologne...just that man scent.

"Here, sit down and let me get you some breakfast. Here's some coffee." He set a steaming hot mug in front of her. "I talked to Sheila, she said Pippa and the puppies are doing great." He handed her a plate of eggs and bacon and gave her a big smile. "It's going to be fun watching those pups grow."

Claire didn't really care about Pippa and her puppies right now...all she could think about was getting naked with Jack. She took a bite of the eggs. "These are good, thank you."

"You're welcome, it's one of the few things I can cook." He kissed her on top of her head before sitting down next to her. "I was happy you had everything in the fridge."

Claire had expected they might spend the night together and had stocked up on some breakfast items. She hadn't expected Pippa to ruin those plans.

"Why do you think you passed out?" Jack asked before taking a bite of eggs.

"I kind of am squeamish about blood and stuff," she said.

Jack just nodded as he looked at her. They ate for a few minutes in silence.

"I'll be back tonight after I close up the store. I have everything we'll need to put up your tree. Also, I can bring dinner if you want me to." He looked at her as he bit into a piece of bacon. His hair had a sexy, tousled look to it.

"That would be nice," she felt her cheeks get warm as she imagined picking up right where they'd left off before the Pippa induced interruption.

"Great...I'll pick something up at Jenny's. I think you're okay to be alone. I haven't seen any evidence of a concussion."

"So, I'm good to resume my normal activities, doctor?" She gave Jack a wink.

"That would be my professional opinion, but then again... I might have a conflict of interest with the patient," he replied, smiling at her.

It was a smile that shot through Claire's core, making her wish she could just pull him to her bedroom and...ravish him.

They finished breakfast together. Jack insisted on doing the dishes before leaving for the hardware store.

* * *

"OH MY GOD, Claire. Are you *okay*?" Emmy asked.

"I'm fine, just an enormous lump on my head and an out-of-control libido."

"That's a relief," Emmy coughed and giggled at the same time.

"Are you laughing at this?" Claire asked, alarmed.

"I'm trying not to, but honestly I can picture the whole thing. I'm just glad you and the puppies are fine," Emmy snickered.

"Ha ha, I'm glad I can amuse you, Em," Claire huffed.

"Seriously, it probably was a good thing that you passed out...otherwise they would have expected you to perform the cutting and tying of the cords."

"Right...good point." She felt queasy again at just the mention of the cords being cut. "What am I doing, Emm? I mean...I'm a *fraud*...and there's no happily ever after with Jack...how would that work with me in L.A. and him in River Falls? *How*?" Claire felt despair come over her. Maybe she should call Jack and cancel tonight. She wasn't sure she could handle any more heartache right now...just put an end to all of this before it got really out of hand.

"Have you given more thought to coming clean with him?" Emmy asked.

"I tried to the other day, I said something about creative license and that I wasn't all that I seemed. But we got interrupted by Beth before I could finish." Claire had a lot of guilt over not being completely honest with Jack. But she wanted so desperately for him, and Beth to have a nice Christmas. She wanted to try her best to help them. Maybe some of what she'd watched Emmy do over the years *had* stuck.

Emmy was quiet for a minute. "You know, Claire, there's no telling how *anything* will ever turn out before we begin something. That's part of the beauty of life. Right? This might lead to heartache...but then again, it might not. Follow your heart and not your head with Jack. You never know what might happen, but you won't find out if you kill it before it's even had a chance to begin."

"Thank you," Claire said softly, letting her friend's words sink slowly into her consciousness. *Let's see where this goes.*

* * *

JACK PULLED in front of Beth's house and killed the engine. Claire had taken up residence in his mind 24/7 lately, and after seeing her naked body last night, he knew she wasn't moving out any time soon. He had been so worked up at the sight of her he'd briefly entertained the thought of telling her Pippa could wait until after they were done. But how would that have looked? She probably would have gotten upset if he'd decided that sex was more important than the dog's wellbeing. *Damn dog.* He walked up to Beth's door in a daze, conjuring up the image of Claire in his arms again, as he let himself in.

"Hey Beth, it's me." Archie immediately shot down the hallway at the sound of Jack's voice. "Hey Arch, let's get you walked." He scratched the small black dog between the ears. Archie immediately rolled onto his back. "Your little shenanigans cost me a lot, buddy," he whispered as he rubbed the dog's stomach.

He stuck his head in Beth's room. "How's it going?" She was scrolling through something on her phone.

"How's it going for *you* is the real question." She set the phone down and looked at Jack. "Sheila told me what happened last night...Claire passed *out*? What happened?"

"Yeah...not sure exactly what happened, but she's okay, and Pippa and the pups are doing well." Jack ran his hand over his jaw. He had a feeling this line of inquiry was going past the normal formalities. He didn't really want to share what Claire had said to him about being squeamish. He was thinking back to when she brought up the issue of creative license. He had been giving it all a lot of thought.

"Hmmm. Sheila also told me you were at Claire's house when she called." Beth's mouth curled at just the hint of a smile.

"Uh...yeah."

"Care to elaborate?"

"Not really...nothing to elaborate on." He glanced at her. When Beth caught wind of something, she didn't let go... kind of like Archie and his favorite bone. "I better get Arch walked," he said as he began to leave the room.

"Archie can wait." At the sound of his name, the dog let out a big snort. "Why *were* you at Claire's last night?"

He was going to have to spill the beans. "We went out on a date. Okay...it was just one date, that's it."

Beth's eyebrows shot up and her eyes grew wide. "I knew it! I could tell there was something between you both. Oh my god, Jack!" Her face was beaming.

"Don't get all worked up...it's not going anywhere...I mean...how could it? She lives there, I live here. End of story."

Archie was looking from Jack to Beth and back to Jack again, as if he too wanted to know how this story was going to end.

"What is meant to be will always find a way, and you guys are so *cute* together." Beth looked as if she were about to burst with happiness.

"You've been reading too many romance novels," he said with a laugh. "Seriously, I better get Archie's walk in, and then I need to head to the store." He took a step towards the hallway.

"Wait, Jack, don't you think it's a bit weird that she passed out? I mean...Sheila said Claire became squeamish, and *that's* why she fainted. What do you think happened?"

Jack scratched his head. "I think she'd probably had too much wine and not enough food at dinner, that's all." Beth seemed satisfied with this.

After getting Archie walked and fed, Jack headed to the store. His thoughts were 100% on Claire, he couldn't wait to resume where they'd left off last night. She was beautiful and his body responded powerfully at the sight of her naked body. He let out a groan at the memory. But there was something else at play...a *different* attraction. He really liked being with her. He felt comfortable around her...but more than just comfortable...he felt as if she belonged...like a missing part of him. Jack had talked little to anyone about Tara. He felt surprised that he'd shared so much of it with Claire. It was a sour memory that he wasn't keen on remembering. But sharing it with her had felt different.

He was really touched to hear about Claire reading to Ruthie at the retirement home. It was really a window into her kindness. It gave his heart a little squeeze.

They'd spent a lot of time together the past week...hours spent at Beth's going through all his dad's stuff. Every memento offered the chance to share a little sliver of himself with Claire, and he'd enjoyed doing it...he didn't usually talk about himself, but with Claire it felt safe and good. They'd both talked about the pain of losing parents. He hadn't really talked much about his dad's passing except with Beth. Claire understood what he was feeling and processing, and he could listen to her as well. He listened to how her parents' death had felt, without trying to fix it. He just listened.

There was a small nagging feeling, though…he wasn't sure what to make of it yet. He normally paid attention to what his gut told him…that intuition had served him well in Afghanistan…most of the time, at least. Something wasn't jiving with Claire. Was it a big deal? He wasn't sure…but he knew something was off…just how big of a something remained to be seen. Maybe she'd feel comfortable enough with him to share whatever the hitch was he was picking up on. Then again, maybe she *had* tried to share something with him, and he hadn't really listened. He kept remembering her words about creative license and "not being all that." Whatever the case was, her help had been invaluable to him, and he was grateful to her.

THE STORE HAD BEEN busy all day, which kept Jack's thoughts and concerns at bay. Before he knew it, it was time to close the store and head over to Claire's. He was gathering the last items he would need for her tree.

"Criminy…"

"What's bugging you, Hank?" Jack smiled to himself as he heard the old veteran grumbling under his breath about something as he locked the door to the store. Something was stirring him up.

"It must be killing Belichick that this kid is so bad at the read-pass option, for Pete's sake…it sure is killing *me*, I'll tell ya that."

"Well, he's no Brady, that's for sure."

"No Brady? Pffft…that's the understatement of the century. Did you see him throw into coverage on third and long last night? Right into the defender's arms…I'm pretty sure he had his eyes closed when he threw it…a high school kid could do better. Patriots won't be making the playoffs, I'll tell ya that." Hank shook his head in resignation before noticing all the stuff Jack was packing up.

"All that for Beth?" he asked, nodding towards the bags Jack had filled.

"Uh…no."

"Are you putting up your *own* tree?" Hank looked incredulous.

"No…it's for Claire."

"You're putting up a tree for Dodger Cap? *I* see." Hank's eyes twinkled as he shoved his hands into his pockets. "Well now…remember…I pointed her out to ya." He rocked back on his feet, a self-satisfied smile across his face. "Don't forget."

"I won't forget." Jack smiled as he headed out to his truck.

CHAPTER 11

*C*laire heard the knock on the door. She checked her reflection in the mirror for what felt like the fiftieth time. *Just relax...you look fine.* But she *couldn't* relax. Her entire insides felt like shifting sand in a molten hot desert. A desert that hadn't seen water in a very long time. She thought her thirst was going to be quenched last night, but it had been a mirage. Pippa wasn't having any more puppies, so nothing was going to get in the way this time. She let out a measured breath between her lips and pulled the door open.

Her heart skipped a beat at the sight of Jack. A flannel shirt over dark jeans, a sexy smile on his face. "Hi," she managed to get out of her dry throat.

"Hi yourself," Jack replied, his hands full of stuff as he gave her a brush of his lips over hers. She felt a jolt of desire shoot through her core.

He cleared his throat, obviously feeling the same thing. "Before you know it, you're going to have a slice of Christmas right here in your living room." He set down several bags. "Just give me a hand with the tree...I'll put it in the stand. If you'll just steady it while I tighten down the screws, that would be great. We'll give it some water and then eat dinner. We can then spend the rest of the night trimming it." Jack coughed a bit, rubbing his hands together, and Claire thought she noticed his face go red.

"Sure...sounds perfect."

Together, they got the tree in the stand and then sat in the dining room to enjoy the food that Jack had picked up at Jenny's.

"That was delicious," Claire said after finishing the turkey meat loaf with mashed potatoes and roasted carrots. Sure beats the frozen stuff I've been eating, she thought.

"Now you see why I eat there so often." Jack gathered up their plates, taking them to the sink. "I bet you're ready to cook your own food." He looked back at her as he ran water over the plates.

"Yeah, I've just been so busy, you know...with all the... stuff." She jumped up quickly and began to unbox the tree lights. She looked over at Jack, who seemed satisfied with her answer. *What are you doing, Claire?* Maybe she should come clean...but then he would know she was a fraud...it would definitely put a damper on what she hoped would happen tonight. Maybe she should wait to say anything. If this was going anywhere, there would be plenty of time to tell him the truth. *Right?*

He joined her in the living room, first getting a fire roaring. They worked together, weaving the string of lights in between the tree's branches; Jack had opted for tiny white ones that twinkled. Then they hung the red glass ornaments. He'd also gotten a box of candy canes they hung on the tree.

"These are a good filler if you don't have a lot of ornaments," he said, holding up one of the red and white striped candies. "You should put that tip in your blog," he said as he pointed it towards her, giving her a sexy smile that made her melt.

"Yeah, that's actually a great idea." She stepped back to admire their work. "It looks beautiful. Thank you."

"Wait, it's not finished." He held up both hands towards her. He used a stepstool from the kitchen to place a shiny gold star on the tree's top. When he stepped down, he snapped off the lights. They both stood and admired the twinkly tree.

Claire inhaled the aroma of pine mixed with the scent of burning oak logs...it was magical and intoxicating. In the darkened room, the tree's lights twinkled brightly, bouncing their reflection against the walls and ceiling. She couldn't help but smile. Jack had come up behind her, placing his hands on her shoulders as she admired the tree. "It's beautiful, Jack...thank you; It really was sweet of you to put up a tree for me." She reached her hands back and held his hands with hers.

"I'm glad you like it," he whispered in her ear, and then kissed her neck. His lips felt warm and tender. His hands moved her hair to one side, allowing him to kiss the sensitive nape area. She let out small whimpers. What he was doing felt good. *Really* good, and her body was responding rapidly. He gently pressed himself against her as he continued. She could feel his desire for her. This sent her insides bolting even more.

She turned towards him, wrapping her arms around his neck. The lights from the tree and fireplace danced in his eyes. She pulled his face to hers and drew him in for a kiss. His arms wrapped tightly around her waist, pulling her against his body. His lips luxurious against hers; soon his tongue gently found its way into her mouth, her insides did somersaults.

Claire stepped back and unbuttoned Jack's flannel shirt. She needed so badly to see him naked in front of her. He finished unbuttoning it and let it drop to the floor. She ran her hands over his shoulders and biceps before pressing herself against him and melting into his lips.

"Maybe you should pull this off," he said in a low voice as he untucked her top and gently pulled it over her head. Claire had on her sexiest lace bra underneath. Jack ran his finger along her collarbone and then slowly down to the swell of her breasts. His finger slipped under the lace and found her nipples, circling them as he kissed her neck. She moaned under his touch, wanting more.

Soon she was lying on the couch watching as Jack undid her jeans, sliding them off her before undoing his own, pulling them to the ground. He laid on top of her, kissing her lips while Claire ran her hands through his soft hair. She buried her nose into him and inhaled his scent while he kissed her neck. Everything about him was intoxicating to her. She wanted every single part of him.

Jack looked up at her. "Is this okay?" he asked.

She could barely squeak out her answer from her dry throat. "Yes."

"Good," he replied before freeing her breasts from her bra and tenderly taking one into his mouth, cupping it gently as he sucked. Slowly, his other hand slid into her panties, cupping her as his tongue worked on her nipples.

Claire was going wild inside; every nerve ending was screaming for more. With his mouth, he slowly worked his way down her stomach, his tongue gliding against her skin. He kissed the outside of her panties before sliding them off her. Gently, he opened her thighs before bringing his mouth to her most sensitive area. *Oh my god this feels so good.*

He alternated between sucking and using his tongue, flicking it lightly against her and making small circles before slipping it inside of her. Claire's breathing became more rapid and ragged as she pulled his head tighter against her as he continued with his mouth. As pleasure came rushing over her, she arched her back and moaned loudly. A tidal wave washed over her. She tingled from the tips of her fingers down to her toes. "Oh Jack, that was so good," she said, breathing heavily.

"Good...there's more to come. You tasted so good in my mouth," he said in a low voice as he stood up. He grabbed a condom from the pocket of his pants.

Claire watched as he slipped out of his jeans and boxers. "Oh my god," she said as her breath caught at the sight of him. He gently laid down on top of her; his body was warm against hers. She ran her hands over his chest and down his arms, feeling the outline of his biceps. Jack let out a groan after gently guiding himself inside of her. She grabbed his shoulders and looked into his eyes. This was not an ordinary roll in the hay. Something more was happening. A connection was clicking into place.

He stopped for a moment and returned her gaze. Without words, they were communicating. His body connected to hers. As he continued, she held onto him tightly. Soon he shuddered with his own release, his face buried in her neck.

He kissed underneath her jaw before finding her lips again. Softly and slowly, he finished what they had begun. He ran his hand over her hair and looked at her. "I hope that was okay."

Claire nodded her head. "It was more than okay...it was pretty spectacular."

Jack smiled. "I agree."

They repeated everything again in the early light of the morning. Claire was giddy with happiness. She was enjoying the moment with little thought about where this was all headed for the time being. They were enjoying a breakfast of coffee and toast before reality came back into sight for her.

"Beth wants to know what the Christmas menu will be. I told her I'd talk to you about it," Jack said.

Ugh. Emmy had given her some ideas for things she would be capable of cooking. "I was thinking a nice honey glazed ham." *Easy...just put in the oven, drizzle with honey, voila.* Claire took a bite of toast, feeling pleased with herself.

"That won't work...Beth is allergic to a preservative used in ham. We were thinking turkey instead."

What? No. Not turkey.

"But didn't you just have turkey for Thanksgiving? Maybe there's ham that isn't preserved." *Good one Claire. Anything but turkey.*

"No...she really can't even stomach the taste of ham because of how sick it makes her. Turkey would be great... we didn't really have one for Thanksgiving because it turned out more like jerky...Beth over-cooked it or the oven was too hot, I can't remember...all I remember was that it tasted like shoe leather. I think we're all hankering for an actual turkey we can eat. Mason's turkey farm is close by. It'll be just like your blog. We can take a visit out there, it's picturesque." He smiled at her, taking a sip of his coffee.

"Great," Claire murmured as she went into full panic mode.

* * *

"ALLERGIC TO HAM? *Who's* allergic to ham?" Emmy's face scrunched up on Claire's phone.

"Beth, that's who. What am I going to do? I can't cook a turkey." Claire had felt her panic turn into despair after Jack left. She was hoping Emmy had a magic solution...like crock pot turkey or something else Claire-proof.

"Don't panic...I'll make a turkey this weekend and video every single step. You can do this Claire...just study the video and memorize the steps. You'll be fine...I'll even write it all out for you. I've got an easy recipe for a beautiful green bean salad that I know you can do…you're great at salads, just make some mashed potatoes and you're golden. You've got this!"

"But I don't, ugh…I don't know Emm…*can* I do this?" Maybe it was time to lay her cards on the table before she really made a fool of herself. Put her tail between her legs and come clean. But what would Jack think of her? He likes the Claire that can bake, sew, and cook…not the totally inept Claire who usually ruined frozen pizza. But then she thought of Jack and Beth and how excited they were to have her help. *How can I let them down?* Maybe she owed it to them to try… they were counting on her to make their Christmas a little special. Maybe she *could* do this with Emmy's help. *Maybe.*

"Think on the bright side…you get to *actually* visit a turkey farm." Emmy's face flashed a big, forced smile. You can take pictures of all the cute, happy turkeys…and an *actual* turkey farmer!"

"Yay, turkey farm," Claire said, her voice completely defeated.

"So, I'm dying to know what happened last night? I think I know because before the subject of turkey came up your face totally was glowing."

Claire's brain went from gloomy to swoony with just the thought of her night with Jack. "It was pretty spectacular, Emm. I can't really explain it…it was great, but something else, there's a weird, connected vibe going on between us. It's as if I've known him so much longer than I actually have. Does that make sense?" She scrunched up her nose, waiting for Emmy to respond.

"It does…it's like when *we* first met…we felt as if we'd been best friends for years. Some people just have that kind of connection. I'm guessing it wasn't exactly like that with Zachary."

"It wasn't…I mean, we connected sexually in an instant.

But I can honestly say that I never really felt that deeper connection with him...I don't think he ever *got* me. It came out when he couldn't handle my grieving. With Jack it's different...*except* he thinks I'm someone I'm not." The reality kept hitting her squarely between the eyes.

"I'm sure that's not why he's attracted to you, Claire, he likes *you*...the actual *you* that's there with him physically... not the you he's reading online*."*

"Maybe," Claire replied glumly.

"Shake yourself out of those thoughts." Emmy smiled at her. "Oh...hey...did you grab extra branches at the tree farm?"

"I did. And I got all the stuff at the craft store you told me to get: wire rings, glue, a pre-tied ribbon, and some small glass ornaments...oh...and pine cones."

"Great. I emailed you step-by-step instructions for the wreath...this is an easy project. Make a practice one for yourself and then make one for Beth. She'll love it."

"Okay, I'll try."

"I also sent you a video and instruction to make a popcorn garland for her tree...it looks *way* more complicated than it is, and it has a pretty big wow factor...another easy project that looks great."

They chatted some more before disconnecting. Claire's thoughts were elsewhere as she gathered everything she needed for the project. Maybe if she could conquer something successfully, she would feel more confident. She'd also felt more like the Claire in the blog. She read Emmy's instructions several times and watched the video she'd made. *Okay, seems kind of doable.*

After about an hour, she stepped back and admired the wreath she had made. Kind of impressive, she thought as she smiled at her handiwork. She'd bent the pine branches around the wire ring, weaving them around as Emmy had shown her. She then glued the glass ornaments and pinecones to the wreath and topped it with a large red satin bow. It was so easy that she'd made the second one for Beth with no problems. Making them had given her a boost of confidence. *Maybe I can do this.* She let the glue dry as she showered and got dressed.

Luckily, the cottage's front door already had a hook to hang the wreath on. She gently placed it on the door and stood back. It looked really good! She snapped a couple of pics of it and sent them to Emmy along with a text.

Claire: Emm...you were right...totally doable...check it out!

Emmy: Beautiful! You can do this...I have faith in you!

Claire felt her mood lift as she admired it. Just then, she got a text from Jack.

Jack: Can you come by Beth's in about an hour? I've got a surprise for you.

Claire: Yay...I love surprises! Can't wait.

She felt totally uplifted and confident. The wreath was beautiful...Beth would love hers *and* Jack had a surprise for her. She could feel her mood lift. Maybe, just *maybe* I can make this all work out, she thought. A feeling of hope surged through her. She went back inside and closed the door. Instantaneously there was the sickening sound of glass hitting brick. She pulled the door open and found all the glass balls smashed on the porch. The pine branches of the wreath had sprung loose from their wire holder and were sticking out all haywire. *Who am I kidding? I can't do this.*

CHAPTER 12

*J*ack had everything organized on Beth's counters. He double checked the list to make sure he hadn't forgotten anything. He hoped Claire was okay with this. *She should be, I mean...how much creative license are we talking about?* Last night had been great. He didn't want to ruin whatever was forming between them. He smiled at the thought of her...how she felt...how she smelled...how she looked. A quiet groan escaped his lips. He'd only had brief flings since his breakup with Tara. No one ever grabbed his attention for very long. Claire had not only grabbed his, but was holding it hostage.

There was that certain something between them. That nub of a feeling you sometimes get when you meet someone new. That feeling of comfort, acceptance, and belonging...all combined with incredible desire and attraction, and, as it turned out, some pretty spectacular chemistry. He could feel the happiness on his face.

"Well, *you* look like all kinds of happy this morning." Beth smiled as she reached for a mug. "Who put the extra sprinkles on *your* donut?"

Jack could feel his face turn hot. "Should you be out of bed? Let me get that...tea or coffee?" He took the mug from her hand; he could feel her eyes boring into his back.

"Well? Does this have something to do with Claire?" she said teasingly. "And what's all this stuff for? Oh my god, is she going to m—"

"It's a surprise...you need to get back to bed, I'll bring you your tea and then I'll take Archie out." The dog ambled into the room and looked up expectantly at Jack before making a loud snort. "Yeah, yeah, you're next buddy." Beth reluctantly returned to her room.

After walking Archie, Jack made sure he had everything that was needed. The knock at the door sent his heart soaring. *She's here.*

He pulled the door open and felt his entire being warm at the sight of her.

"Hi," he said as he let her in. He leaned down and kissed her softly on her lips, immediately wanting more. *Think cold shower.*

"Hi," she replied, taking off her coat. Her cheeks were pink from the cold weather and her eyes were warm. "Was that the surprise?" She winked at him.

"Do you want it to be?" he said in a low voice. Jack's body was heating up at the thought.

"Maybe," she replied, a sly look on her face.

"Just *maybe*? Wow...I better work on my skills." He made an exaggerated slump of his shoulders.

"Trust me...your skills are top notch." Her brown eyes held his.

"I'll be sure to put them to use again...soon." He cleared his throat. "But first things first...come this way." He motioned for her to follow him into the kitchen.

Jack strategically had his back against the counter, hiding everything. He stepped aside with a flourish. "Surprise!"

Claire stared at the bags of flour and sugar, the rolling pin, cookie sheets and numerous spices with a blank look in her eyes.

"Gingerbread house time!" He waited for her response. He'd swear that a look of horror washed over her. "I know you said you wouldn't have time to make your annual Christmas gingerbread house...but Beth *really* had her heart set on one...I thought we could do it together. I've got carpentry skills, you've got the baking skills, so... I should be of *some* help...right?"

She just stood there, silently nodding her head. The flush that had been in her cheeks had vanished. "Claire...are you all right?" *Shit...I screwed up with this idea.*

She shook her head. "No...you're right...this will be fine...totally fine, I've got this." He saw her take a gulp. "You *can* help...*right?*"

"Of course, just tell me what to do. I read your blog, got all the ingredients for baking and decorating, and everything else I figured you'd need. I thought it would be fun. You know...just me and you...together." He smiled at her... pulling her in for a kiss. God, she tasted good. He had every intention of helping, but it was going to be hard to stay focused. All he could think of was getting her back in to bed again. And again. *Cold shower time, Jack.* "I even made the templates for you; I used the dimensions given in your blog...it's all ready to go."

Claire just stood silently. Nodding in agreement as she put an apron on over her head.

"I need to cover the store for about an hour while Hank runs an errand. I figured that'll give you time to make the dough and get the pieces into the oven...after they've cooled, we can assemble everything." The color was still missing from her face. "I've walked Archie, so he shouldn't be a problem." She still looked stricken. "I won't be long...promise, and when I'm back we'll do the rest together." He kissed her on the top of her forehead...he didn't want to keep thinking about cold showers.

* * *

"EMM WHAT AM I going to do?" Claire said, her voice just above a whisper...she didn't want Beth to hear her losing her shit. She was in full on panic mode over the gingerbread house. *Surprise*? It was more like a nightmare.

"Calm down...the baking part isn't that hard. Follow the recipe...it's just mixing the ingredients, that's all."

"And then what??? It's got to be more than just mixing ingredients," Claire hissed.

"Once it's mixed, chill the dough and then roll it out... easy...the secret is to use enough flour so that the rolling pin doesn't stick, if it begins to stick too much even with flour, throw it back into the fridge. Once you have it rolled out, you'll use the template to cut out the pieces of the house, then carefully transfer them on to the baking sheet, chill in the freezer for fifteen minutes and then bake. Seriously. This is the easy part, Claire. It's the building and decorating that I'm worried about."

"You and me both. I mean...Jack *does* build things...maybe this is pretty much the same. Except...how are we sticking everything together...I'm sure it's not with nails." Claire was trying not to panic but it wasn't working.

"Icing, the icing is used to glue it together."

"*Icing*? I've got to make that too?" she wailed. She needed to sit down. There was no way in hell she was going to be able to pull this off.

"Here's my advice...go to the store and buy some pre-made icing. Just tell Jack it's a quick tip...no one's going to be eating the house so it's a way to cut corners."

99

That'll work, thought Claire. She'd get the icing while the gingerbread was baking.

"Call me if you need help…or text if you can't call. You've got this Claire."

Claire wished she had as much confidence in herself as Emmy did. She pulled up the recipe on her phone, read it a few times before beginning to make the dough.

* * *

As CLAIRE LOOKED DOWN at the baking sheets, she felt a swell of pride. Making the gingerbread house pieces had felt like a roller coaster ride. One minute she was in a giant dip of despair, the next minute at the peak of elation. Currently, she was high in the air and hoping the ride was over. The gingerbread pieces were all laid out neatly on two cookie sheets. She was feeling quite happy with herself, although just 20 minutes earlier she'd been clutched with panic and feelings of failure. She pushed the cookie sheets into the hot oven, removed her apron and grabbed her purse.

Claire stuck her head in Beth's room. "I'm running to the store, is there anything you need me to grab for you?" Beth was propped up in bed reading a book. She quickly threw the book to the side, a huge smile spreading across her face, she tucked a blond curl behind one ear.

"No, I'm fine. But a little birdie told me that you and Jack went on a date." Her face was lit up as if Christmas had come early.

"Yeah, but…it was just one date." Claire was trying to play it cool.

"I heard that he was at *your* place the night the puppies came," Beth said, still looking excited.

Wow, news really does travel fast here, thought Claire. "I…well…he was helping me with my Christmas tree." Claire could feel her cheeks burn; she wasn't used to everyone not only knowing her business but talking about it too.

"I've noticed how you both are around each other…I can tell it's something more than just a date going on." She patted the bed for Claire to sit down.

"There's really nothing to talk about, Beth. I'm going back to L.A. after New Year's…so…there's nothing *there*." Claire sat down at the end of the bed, Archie had plopped down next to her, all four feet in the air expecting a belly rub. Claire complied, rubbing the dog's stomach.

"Oh…don't give me that…you write a blog for a living… you could do that *anywhere*."

"Beth…you are totally putting the cart before the horse here…I mean…I've only known Jack for a couple of weeks." Beth was right…she could write the blog from any location… except for the fact that the heart of it…Emmy…lived in Los Angeles…that was the piece of the puzzle Beth was missing. And she was getting ahead of herself here…there was a connection between her and Jack…a pretty powerful one… but it was *way* too soon to be thinking of a relationship. *Or was it?* Because just the thought of him made her entire being feel happy.

"Jack doesn't just go out with women willy nilly, Claire. He hasn't been interested in anyone since college…since—"

"—Tara…I know, he told me about her. I just…" Claire wanted to spill her guts to Beth…but couldn't…not without revealing she was a fraud…not who she seemed to be. "…it's just, I think it's too soon. And…I'm not leaving L.A…it's all I've known," she said quietly.

She gathered her coat and purse and darted over to River Falls Grocery. She replayed in her mind the conversation with Beth. She had been kind of surprised to hear that Jack hadn't shown an interest in anyone since Tara. Had Jack talked to Beth about her? Or had Beth put two and two together on her own? And did any of it matter...because she wasn't moving from L.A. and Jack wasn't leaving River Falls...and the elephant in the room was that Claire wasn't the Claire he thought she was. Her head was cautious and confused but her heart was falling for him...and fast. She told herself to set aside her concerns for the time being and enjoy all the good feelings he was giving her right now. *All of them.*

She grabbed the cans of frosting and made her way back to Beth's. The gingerbread should be done by then, she thought. Hopefully Jack would be waiting for her when she got back. She couldn't wait to see him. Thinking about being back in his arms made her entire body feel warm, despite the frigid temperatures outside.

Jack's truck *was* there when she pulled up. She made her way to the door as she mapped out the evening in her head. They'd let the gingerbread cool...probably overnight would be a good idea. They could then head back to her place, and—

Jack opened the front door as she approached.

"Hi," she said, beaming at him.

"You'd better come look at the gingerbread," he said, a worried look on his face.

What? Her roller coaster had climbed the peak and now was headed downhill at about a hundred miles an hour and was about to go completely off the tracks. Claire looked at the cookie sheets. The gingerbread shapes were gone. The carefully cut out pieces had melted and combined into one giant liquidy blob...there was no resemblance of a house at all.

"Oh no...what happened?" Claire wailed. She'd followed the instructions to a tee. "Maybe it's the oven?" she cried.

Archie had let out a loud snort from his bed in the corner.

"I don't think the oven would cause *this*," Jack replied,

motioning to the mess on the cookie sheets. "I have an idea though...maybe we can cut the shapes out once these have cooled." He had a hopeful expression on his face.

"Good idea," Claire replied. She was going over everything she'd done, trying to figure out what could have gone wrong. She wasn't a baker, so literally it could have been anything. *I can't do this.* She'd worked so hard on this and thought she'd done a good job. Obviously not.

Jack took her hand. "Hey, it's okay...it's only gingerbread." He leaned down to smile at her. "I know what can cheer you up...how about we go to Jenny's and grab something to eat. I got a text a bit ago saying she's got apple pie. Would pie help?" He raised his eyebrows expectantly as he put his arms around her shoulders, giving her a gentle squeeze. Claire nodded as she tried to hold back tears. She was trying her best, and it just wasn't cutting it. "And when we get back, maybe this'll be ready for us to work on. I think it'll probably be fine...just needs to cool...and solidify."

"Okay. Pie sounds good," she sniffled.

He took her hand in his as they walked out to his truck. Just that simple touch and connection to Jack's body made her feel better.

She slid into the booth at Jenny's, the smell of home cooking and the sight of the fire going in the corner made her feel warm and a bit happier. They'd both ordered the clam chowder...it was warm and delicious. The homemade bread that accompanied it was soft and chewy. Claire loved being in Jack's company. He was easy for her to talk to. He made her laugh, and he was sexy as hell. There was such an easy way about the two of them together. She had been climbing upwards once more, hopeful that all the gingerbread needed was a good cooling down.

"Tell me, how big of a Sox fan *are* you?" Claire said. Their pies and coffee had just arrived.

"So…this is where the *real* hiccup is…not the fact that you live three thousand miles away…but the fact that I'm a Sox fan." Jack smiled before taking a bite of apple pie and ice cream.

"A girl's gotta have her priorities straight…I mean… c'mon, we're talking baseball here."

"Well, I'm not as crazy as Hank is if that's what you're asking. But my dad and I would attend several Sox games a year together. It's one of my fondest memories of him, and one thing I'm going to miss the most. I kind of can't imagine heading to Fenway without him."

Claire reached across the table and placed a hand over his. "I'm so sorry, Jack. I know how hard that must be. It's great though, that you have these memories of him…those special times will live forever in your heart."

He looked up; his blue eyes were damp. "Thank you, I know you get it." He placed his other hand on hers, giving it a gentle squeeze. He took a bite of his pie and then looked up at her, his eyes twinkling. "So, to go back to your question… the Red Sox are my team…I've been attending games at Fenway since I could walk…I've taken the Fenway tour a dozen times and every time I see that red seat where in 1946 Ted Williams hit his 502-foot home run, I still get goosebumps."

"How amazing! I'm not a Sox fan, but that is baseball history." Claire smiled at him. "I love baseball so much…to me spring equals baseball."

"I totally agree. Nothing better than baseball." Jack took a sip of his coffee before continuing. "So, let's pretend that if we were together—"

Claire stopped mid-bite and raised an eyebrow at him.

"—just pretending…and the Sox were facing the Dodgers in the World Series…I'd be all in on the Sox if that's what you're asking…that's how big of a fan I am."

"Okay…that's fair enough…but…what if…just pretending here," she winked at Jack, "we were together, and the Dodgers were in the World Series, against any team *except* the Sox, who would you be pulling for?" She put her fork down as she waited for his reply.

"Anybody but the Dodgers."

"What?!? Then I'd say you're *just* as crazy as Hank. If the shoe were on the other foot, *I'd* be rooting for the Sox because *you'd* be rooting for the Sox. What do you say to that?"

"I'd say you were a fair weathered Dodger fan," he teased.

"It's a good thing this is just pretend, then." *And it is just pretend, Claire.* But what about what Beth had said? Maybe it wasn't pretend for Jack.

"Yeah…good thing," he replied, before taking another bite of pie. Claire thought she caught a brief look of sadness cross his face.

They finished their pies and coffee and headed back to Beth's. Claire hoped that the gingerbread was going to be okay. But after two hours of cooling, it hadn't solidified and was *far* from being okay. It was a soft, doughy mess. She told Jack she had a headache and went home.

She'd been on the couch with her eyes closed for the past hour. Emmy had taken Nona to a doctor's appointment and would call her as soon as she was back. Claire felt like a failure and a fraud. She was afraid that if Jack discovered the truth about her, he'd no longer be interested, which was ironic because the only reason she'd put herself in this position in the first place, was because she wanted to be near him. She let out a big sigh.

CHAPTER 13

"Oooh...it smells so good in here...I know what you're up to!" Beth walked excitedly into the kitchen as Jack was scraping the remains of the failed gingerbread into the trash.

"Wait...what happened?" Beth looked around the room in puzzlement. "Where's the gingerbread house?"

"There isn't one," Jack said. He grabbed the second cookie sheet and shoveled its contents into the trash bin. "For some reason it didn't come out right."

"Where's Claire?" Beth still looked confused as she surveyed the mess in the kitchen.

"Home." He didn't really feel like playing twenty questions with Beth. He had a few questions of his own. *How much creative license are we talking about?*

"Is she coming back?"

"Nope. Not tonight, at least. She's got a headache. You should get back into bed. I'll make tea for you, and I'll make sure this is all cleaned up before I leave. When's Tyler back?" He was trying his best to get her off the Claire topic.

"He's driving back tomorrow." She still had a furrowed

brow, and Jack could see her trying to make sense of the situation.

"Did you tell him he's helping me with the outdoor lights when he gets back?"

Beth appeared to snap out of whatever thoughts had been bothering her. "Yeah, I told him. He said no problem...he's grabbing some seafood to bring back...said he's making his seafood stew. He wants you to stay for dinner, you guys can do the lights then."

"Great...sounds good." Whenever Tyler was in Boston on business, he'd stop and get fresh seafood on his way back to River Falls, often making his signature stew with it.

"Do you think Claire would like to come, too? I'm sure she would love to be part of the big moment when you turn the lights on," Beth said.

Jack had helped his dad put up Christmas lights whenever he was home from Afghanistan. When he wasn't around, Tyler had helped. His dad had tried stubbornly to do it himself, but after a small fall one year, he'd grudgingly conceded that maybe he shouldn't be up on a ladder anymore. He'd always gone all out, covering nearly every square inch of the home's roof with colorful lights. Their house had always been one of the most festive and brightly lit ones in the neighborhood. Jack was going to make sure it was every bit as nice this year.

"Sure...I'll ask her." He shuttled Beth back to bed and made her a cup of tea before tackling the mess in the kitchen. Finally, he walked Archie, told Beth goodnight, and headed back to his house. His thoughts had been on Claire the entire time. He felt disappointed when she had left. They'd had such a nice dinner together, but when she saw the gingerbread, she looked completely defeated. She'd said she had a headache and abruptly left.

Jack didn't question that she wasn't feeling well. But

something felt off. It felt as if she wasn't telling him something. He was beginning to have an idea what that something was, and frankly he didn't care. He just wished she trusted him enough to confide in him. Despite this, he couldn't get around the fact that she had stolen his heart, something that hadn't happened since Tara. He not only found her sexy as hell, but adorable. They shared a common interest in their love of baseball. And she was sweet. He loved her stories about Ruthie. It was clear to him that she had a good heart, something that Jack valued greatly.

Jack liked that he could open up to her about his dad. She'd been empathic and kind as she listened to him. In return, he'd listened to her. He never questioned her feelings; he'd only listened and offered support. He had a strong desire to protect and take care of her. Days were always brighter when she was around. All of this outweighed the questions that had arisen; whatever those were, they weren't important to him. He risked the possibility that she'd return to L.A. and forget about him. He had to take that risk though. His heart had informed him that there wasn't any other option.

And, their intimacy had only confirmed what his heart had begun to feel. He'd known he was in rare territory the minute he'd looked into her brown eyes while they were in bed together. That place in his heart that had been lost for many years had awoken. Jack wanted to be around her every day and every night. *Every* single solitary night…wrapped up in his arms. He knew. He just knew. She checked all his boxes. But *how* was he going to make it all work? He didn't know. He was still working that out. But he knew he *needed* to work it out. He needed her.

* * *

CLAIRE REACHED for her buzzing phone.

"Hi Emm...before I unload about my pit of despair... how's Nona?"

"Oh no...I'm guessing it didn't go well with the ginger-bread. Nona is fine...the doctor increased one of her medications. Hopefully they can get her blood pressure under better control. I took her out to lunch afterwards; we had a pleasant time."

"I'm glad she's okay."

"Me too. Now tell me what happened to the gingerbread? Why didn't you call me for help?"

"It was going fine, that's why...I had the shapes on the cookie sheets...they looked perfect, Emm...but, for some reason, they all melted into one giant pan of soft dough. I even let it cool off, hoping I could just cut the shapes out afterwards, but it was so crumbly that it was impossible. You should have seen the look on Jack's face, Emm...he *knows* I'm a fraud, I *am* a fraud." She began to chew on her bottom lip.

"Everything will be okay. I wish I was there to help you."

"Me too," Claire said. "Jack must know I'm not real. I've been dropping hints...and now this."

"Well...any number of things can go wrong when baking even to the best of us. If it was soft, it could have been too much baking powder...did you use just the one teaspoon, like the recipe says?"

"I did."

"And you're sure it was the teaspoon that you used... because it sounds like too much baking powder caused it to be soft."

"Uh huh, I remember only putting one in...the teaspoon's the big one, right?"

"Oh my god, no Claire...that's the *tablespoon*...no wonder it didn't turn out...you used *three times* the amount the recipe calls for. Okay...no worries, now you know what you did wrong...just make it again but use the small spoon next time."

"Honestly, Emm, I don't have the energy or the time to do it again. Beth has a list a mile long of errands and projects she needs Jack and I to do.

"Then just tell her something wasn't right and tough luck on the gingerbread house."

"I don't know...maybe I *can* try again...tomorrow. I'll be back over there; we're getting all the outdoor lights organized...I think Beth's husband will be back from a business trip to help Jack put them up. Maybe while they're doing that I can try again." A small sliver of hope had re-lodged itself back into Claire's heart. She desperately wanted to help Jack and Beth. *Maybe I can do this after all.*

But what was *this*? Was it the whole Christmas thing? Or was it the entire relationship thing? *Relationship*? How would that even be possible? She needed to tell him...part of her *needed* to. Maybe Emmy was right...maybe it was other qualities that Jack found attractive. But it was the skills she pretended to have that brought them together in the first place. Was everything built on lies and falsehoods?

She sighed as she settled onto the couch and re-read her gingerbread house blog.

A GINGERBREAD HOME for the Holidays

When I was growing up, nothing said Christmas more than my mom's annual tradition of building a beautiful gingerbread house. Every year she would create a charming home made of gingerbread, decorated with icing and candies. The house sat front and center on our entry hall table, greeting visitors with a very merry Christmas. It filled our home with the warm spiced scent of the season.

Now, I can hear many of you saying, 'there's no way in *bleep*

I can do that.' I am here to say that you can! The steps for baking the pieces couldn't be easier. I've attached a step-by-step set of instructions. Once the house is built, you can let your creative energy loose and decorate it to your heart's desire, really no design or idea is off limits. Maybe try to replicate your family home or even build an alpine cottage. Get creative! There is a gingerbread house making goddess inside of you! Now get baking!

JACK AND CLAIRE spent the next week working on various projects. Jack was happy to be distracted from the mess the hardware store was in financially; spending time with Claire was preferable to trying to figure out how to keep the store afloat.

Jack and Tyler had tackled the outdoor lights. Claire was present to witness the final plug-in…it was a tradition his dad had begun; he would wait until after dinner before gathering everyone outside to watch as he turned the lights on. It put a smile on Jack's face, having Claire there to share in the occasion. She made him feel hopeful that maybe Christmas wouldn't be as rough as he'd expected it to be.

Claire's second attempt at the gingerbread house had been successful. At least she'd been able to bake the pieces properly. Jack would be lying if he didn't admit that her skills at decorating the house weren't quite up to par, but Jack's skills in making birdhouses had come in handy and it had turned out not half bad. After an initial look of surprise, Beth had clapped at the sight of it, and pulled both Claire and Jack in for a big hug.

In between all their projects and errands, he and Claire had carved out some time for themselves. Surprisingly, they hadn't had snow yet this year, which was unusual…climate change in action evidently. Jack wanted to take Claire cross-country skiing, or snow shoeing, but without snow they'd settled for some hikes; the air was usually bitter cold, but the skies had been clear and blue. He'd enjoyed this time with her. She made him smile and laugh. There had been a lot of good-natured teasing about baseball; Claire was easy to be around. The chemistry between them had been the cherry on top. His heart was becoming more and more enamored with the adorable and sexy Claire.

They'd been able to spend a few nights together over the past week. Each time they had been intimate, it felt as if they were being drawn closer together. Jack's entire body desired to be with her as much as possible. They fit together perfectly and seemed in complete harmony, sexually. The connection between them had only grown stronger. Jack was doing his level best to put off thinking about what would happen once the holidays were over. He and Claire hadn't spoken a word out loud about the issue, but it was clear, it was on each of their minds.

Tomorrow, they were going to spend part of the day at Mason's Turkey Farm. He'd thought he saw a bit of a freak-out cross Claire's face when he first mentioned it, but she soon seemed calmer, saying she looked forward to taking some pictures for the blog. Masons would be perfect for that; it was complete with a red barn and everything.

For now, he was stuck once again, trying to make sense of his dad's bookkeeping methods. He was also turning over different ideas and ways to bring more business to the store. One option was to have an online presence, something his dad had waived away as "too high-tech and fancy," but Jack was considering any and all options right now. Anything to hang on to the family business. For himself, Beth, and for the town. He just hoped it was possible.

* * *

"IT'S GETTING to be crunch time." The worry on Emmy's face was crystal clear, even over Claire's small phone screen. "What's your plan?"

Claire had been agonizing over this herself. What *was* her plan? Jack had stolen her heart. She loved spending time with him, whether it was on one of their many hikes, running one of Beth's endless errands, or when they were in each other's arms having the best sex Claire had ever had. But where was this going? Christmas was just a few days away and yet she'd remained silent…keeping her secret to herself. That was just the first problem. She had agonized over how to come clean. She was wracked with guilt but ultimately felt that she was helping Jack and Beth; the time had never seemed right to say anything. The other issue was how to make an L.A. to River Falls romance work. *Could* she leave L.A.?

Putting aside the issue of her partnership with Emmy, Claire wasn't sure she could imagine herself being a small-town girl. She'd lived in Los Angeles her entire life. Yes, the traffic was a major pain in the ass…yes, the smog was really awful some days…yes, the earthquakes, and the fires, and the droughts weren't a lot of fun either, but it was *L.A.;* home to hundreds of different cultures, all coming together in one big and beautiful melting pot. As charming as River Falls was, and it *was* charming, and there was something about knowing everyone had your back if you needed help…but it was missing some of what she loved about Los Angeles. There were none of the shops run by new immigrants selling all kinds of wonderful and unique items, or the cultural festivals, and there weren't the variety of ethnic foods Claire had grown up with. She realized each place had its own pros and cons, and maybe she could sacrifice these things for a life with Jack. This brought her full circle to square one: her business partner was three thousand miles away and she didn't know how Jack would react to the *real* Claire.

"Well? What's your plan?" Emmy's eyebrows rose as she waited for Claire to respond.

"I have nothing, Emm…nothing. I have no idea what to do or how to make any of this work. And on top of that, I'm stressing over the whole turkey cooking thing. We're going to a turkey farm tomorrow…which I guess will be kind of fun…I can get some pics, and now I'll have *really* been to one, instead of just reading about it online. Maybe the opportunity to talk to Jack will present itself tomorrow. He said it's about a thirty-minute drive. Maybe it's time…I'm just frightened, Emm." Claire felt the fear in her chest. It terrified her that her revelation might scare Jack away…she hadn't been honest with him. How was he going to feel about that?

"It'll be okay," Emmy said softly. "You didn't plan any of this…it just happened. But you *do* need to tell him."

Claire was silent as she nodded her head in agreement. She just hoped Jack saw it that way, too.

CHAPTER 14

*C*laire had her mind on whether this was the right time to reveal herself to Jack. They were on their way to Mason's Turkey Farm, about thirty-minutes away. Jack had told her to bundle up as it was brisk outside. She'd donned her warmest coat and added her scarf, hat, and mittens.

She looked over at Jack as he drove. He looked hot as usual in a flannel shirt over a white t-shirt. A red beanie pulled over his head. What would his reaction be when he found out she wasn't the real deal? Would he be angry? Hurt? Would he still be attracted to her? These thoughts swirled in her mind. As she continued to stare at him, he broke out into a big grin.

"I can feel your eyes on me," he said, looking straight ahead.

"I was just thinking," she replied. Her stomach in knots.

"I've been thinking too." He glanced over at her before returning his eyes to the road. "I could use your advice about something."

What is this about? "Sure…I'm all ears."

"I've been really wracking my brain trying to find a solution for the store…it's not doing well, hasn't been for a while."

"I'm sorry, Jack." Claire reached out and touched him on the arm. "I know how much it means to you."

"For all of dad's great qualities, running a business wasn't one of them. I'm trying to figure out how to keep it afloat. I don't want to lose it. It's important not only to me and Beth, it's our legacy really, but it's important to the town…at least to those who haven't taken their business to one of the giants." He ran a hand over his face, remaining silent for a moment. "I was thinking of investing in a website." He glanced over at her. "I'm just not sure whether that will help…and the cost of getting someone to build one won't be cheap."

Claire was nodding her head. "It's a step in the right direction, but you're right, you need more than just a website."

"That's what I keep coming back to as well."

They were silent for a few minutes. Claire looked out the window and watched as farms, dotted with sheep and horses flanked by gentle rolling hills, sped by. "You could try writing a blog." She looked over at Jack.

"A blog? Like what you do?"

"Yeah…except you would use it to direct traffic to your website, or into the store for sales."

Jack lowered his brows. "I'm not really seeing how that would work." He glanced over at her briefly before returning his eyes to the road.

"Let's say you blogged about a project…such as your bird houses…that's it Jack," Claire clapped her mittened hands together, "you could blog about building birdhouses, you know…a DIY project, and then direct your readers to the store for all the materials they would need...ohhh...you could even offer kits...everything ready to go to build the bird house in one box." She smiled and her eyes lit up as she continued to think out loud. "Maybe you could even ramp up to playhouses and doll houses."

Jack nodded his head. "But how do I get people to even *find* the blog...it would be like a needle in a haystack, right?"

"You'd need a social media presence. That's how I launched *City Meets Country*, I blasted beautiful photos with hashtags all over social media. Little by little people began to follow...you direct them to the blog which then—"

"—directs them to the store's website, where they hopefully make a purchase."

"Exactly!" Claire felt really excited...this was right up her alley, and she knew it could be successful, the birdhouses were *so* adorable, scaling them larger into doll houses and playhouses wouldn't be that hard.

"Except I wouldn't be able to write a blog. And social media? Yeah...don't think I'm going to be able to do that either." Jack had pulled onto a winding road which led to a red barn and fenced area with what appeared to be hundreds of turkeys running around. On the side of the barn "Mason's Turkey Farm" was painted in big white letters.

"But *I* know how to do those things," she said excitedly.

Jack was silent for a minute before replying. "Except you're leaving." He looked over at her, his mouth set in a firm line as he got out of the truck.

Right. I'm leaving. Claire sat for a second, trying to sort out her thoughts. *Am I leaving?* She opened the truck's door and climbed out. Jack had walked over to a tall man wearing overalls and a barn coat.

"Claire, this is Henry Mason, this farm has been in his family for generations. He and my dad were good friends."

"Hi," Claire shook the farmer's hand. "This is beautiful.

Oh my gosh…how many turkeys are out here?" She watched them roaming around their fenced-in area.

"We raise about a hundred turkeys a year."

"They all look so happy…out in the fresh air with lots of room to run around." The sight of the turkeys strutting and pecking at the ground was exactly as Claire pictured.

"We feed them only organic foods, all the grasses and berries here are treated without pesticides."

"That's awesome," Claire replied. "Healthy turkeys." She smiled excitedly.

"Feel free to walk around, let me know if you have any questions. Good to see you, Jack." The farmer shook Jack's hand.

"I'm going to get some terrific pictures." Claire felt inspired as she snapped pictures of the turkeys, their barn, and the beautiful countryside. The clean crisp air filled her lungs. You certainly didn't get this kind of air in L.A.

"I was surprised you hadn't included any photos on your blog from your turkey farm visit." Jack had taken one of her hands in his.

"I think I had camera trouble that day," Claire murmured. *Shit, Claire…another lie.*

They walked quietly hand in hand.

"I think your ideas for the store are really good." He looked at her, giving her hand a squeeze. "I just don't think…scratch that…I *know* that I don't have the skill set for it."

"But *I* do, Jack…and before you point out the fact that I'm leaving…it *could* work. There's no reason in the world why I couldn't do it remotely from Los Angeles."

"How are you going to take pictures remotely?" He stopped walking and looked at her.

"I'm sure you can take pictures, Jack. Really." *Why is he putting up obstacles that aren't there?*

"Well sure…I can…but I've seen your blog and social media…you take fantastic pictures."

Claire finished with her camera and looked over at Jack. He had his hands shoved in his pockets…a look on his face that Claire couldn't quite decipher.

They continued to walk, making a big loop around the entire farm, ending up back in front of the barn where Henry was waiting for them.

"Well, I think I've got a lot of good shots…I'm ready to go anytime you are." She looked over at Jack, before turning her attention to the farmer. "It was really nice meeting you, thank you for showing us your farm; the turkeys are simply adorable." Claire held her hand out to the old man.

"Aren't you going to pick one out?" He scratched his head with one hand as he shook Claire's outstretched hand with the other.

"Pick one out for what?" she asked, feeling puzzled. Jack was looking at her with a bewildered look on his face.

"To be slaughtered, of course," the farmer replied.

"*Slaughtered*?" Claire shrieked. Her eyes went from Jack to the farmer and back to Jack again.

"Just pick one out for us, Henry," Jack said.

"City people…where do they *think* their food comes from?" the farmer mumbled as he walked off, shaking his head.

"Jack…he's going to *slaughter* a turkey for us?" Claire felt her throat tighten.

"Of course…what did you think we were going to do… take it to a movie? Didn't you pick one out before?"

Claire was pretty sure that Emmy had picked theirs out at Whole Foods. A horrible feeling began in her stomach, making its way up to her chest.

"We…we… *we* could get a *Tofurkey* instead," she pleaded.

"A toe *what*?" Jack looked at her as if she'd sprouted horns.

"A Tofurkey…you know…a turkey made from tofu." She was nodding her head quickly, eyebrows raised, her mittened hands clasped together. *Oh please.*

"A turkey… made of *tofu*? Seriously?" Jack looked incredulous before clearing his throat. "I'm pretty sure Marty doesn't carry those at the market."

"But…but…we—" Just then there was the sickening sound of a turkey screeching loudly; a split second later everything went silent.

"Well…I think it's a moot point now," Jack said.

"Oh no," Claire wailed. She buried her face in Jack's chest. "Poor turkey," she sobbed.

CLAIRE HELD the bag containing the turkey on her lap as they drove back to River Falls in silence. Every few minutes a shudder would wrack her shoulders and her eyes would well up with tears that would then roll slowly down her cheeks. And even though she wasn't intrinsically religious, she prayed for the turkey's soul all the way home before breaking out in another sob. *I should become a vegetarian.*

Jack had tried to console her. He looked puzzled by her reaction. He seemed to be trying to make her feel better, but it wasn't working.

"I'm confused…I mean…you visited a turkey farm before…you've written about *cooking* turkeys on your blog… I've seen you *eat* turkey at Jenny's. I don't understand where all the tears are coming from." He reached out and put an arm around her. "What's up?"

She tried to speak without sobbing. Maybe something more *was* going on here. Was it hormones? It was close to that time of the month. Was it the stress from the fact that she was falling for this man, but her life was three thousand miles away? Was it her guilt over not telling him yet? *What's going on?* Maybe all those things had combined into the perfect storm today. She continued to let out a sob every few minutes until Jack pulled up in front of her house.

"Do you want me to stay with you?" His face was full of concern. "I'm a very good comforter, you know. I could make you some tea...stay with you until you're feeling better, or even all night if that's what you wanted."

Claire shook her head no. She said something about wanting some time to herself before slipping out of the truck. Jack walked her to the door and kissed her lightly on the head before saying goodbye.

* * *

"Emm it was *horrible*! I caused a turkey to die," Claire said into the phone's screen. She was wracked with guilt over what had happened.

Emmy screwed up her face. "Uh...what did you *think* was going to happen, Claire? I mean...you *were* at a turkey farm... turkey *is* on the menu. Seriously, what were you thinking?"

"Oh, don't look at me like that. I'm not sure *what* I was thinking, but I didn't think we were going to commit turkey homicide."

"But that's were turkeys come from...even the ones from Whole Foods."

"I know—" Claire let out a shuddered breath. "I feel responsible for Tom's death." She wiped a tear from her cheek.

"Tom? Claire, please tell me you didn't give the turkey a name."

She was nodding her head. "I did. I don't know Emm... you're right, I *should* have expected that was going to happen.

What's wrong with me? I'm a big bundle of nerves the past few days."

"I think you know where it's coming from. I'm guessing you didn't tell him yet?"

"No, I didn't. We got to talking about his business, and some ideas to make it profitable. Emm…I could totally help him." Claire relayed to Emmy the ideas she and Jack had discussed.

"Claire, that's a brilliant idea. You could *totally* make that work. That pic you sent me of the birdhouse was adorable! Of course, those would sell…either pre-made or as kits. And you're right, easy to scale up to doll houses and playhouses, they probably have everything needed already in stock."

"Right? It's really a brilliant plan. But I'm going back in a couple of weeks…how does that work?"

"Well, everything you've laid out could be done from here."

"I know. But then I wouldn't be near *him*." Claire peeked up at her friend.

Emmy's face smiled and it looked as if something had just dawned on her. "You're falling in love with him."

Claire just nodded her head and let out a big sigh. "I might be. It's crazy, *right*? We've only known each other a few weeks."

"No, not crazy at all. My parents met, fell in love, and got married in just a couple of months…look at *them*. They've been married for thirty-five years. My dad always says, 'when you know, you know.' Do you think Jack feels the same?"

"I think so…but he doesn't know who I *really* am."

"He knows the person he spends time with, Claire. That's all that matters."

"I hope you're right." Claire bit her lip. *I hope you're right.*

CHAPTER 15

*B*eth squealed with delight as Jack handed her the carton of ice cream.

"Best brother ever...hands down." She closed her eyes as she spooned in the chocolate treat. "Marty will probably be happy when he no longer needs to order this by the case."

"You think that will stop once you give birth? If I remember correctly, you've always loved that flavor."

"Yeah, but I wasn't eating three pints of it a week," she snorted before putting the carton down on her nightstand. "What's up, Jack? I can tell something is on your mind."

Beth had always had a sixth sense when anything was bothering him, no matter how well he tried to disguise it. When they were kids, she'd instinctively known when he'd had a bad day at school or if a girl had broken his heart. She rarely said anything. She'd just put her arm around him and give him a hug and he would know she was there for him. But when their dad died, they both had needed support. Jack had tried his best to console Beth but had needed his own comfort. It was part of the reason that he felt so powerfully connected to Claire, she'd offered that support to him.

"It's Claire. Something doesn't add up...and I'm not sure it really matters to be honest." He rubbed the back of his neck and sat down at the end of the bed, Archie ambled over and flopped down next to him.

Beth looked at him quizzically. "What doesn't add up?"

"It's as if she's a different person from who she is online." He looked over at his sister while scratching Archie's ears.

"I think that's probably normal that people are not *exactly* the same as their public presence...don't you?"

"No...I mean, yeah...I agree with that. But this is more...if I didn't know any better, I'd say she's practically cooked nothing in her life. When we made the gingerbread house, it was as if she'd never done it before, and then at the turkey farm today...she just kind of lost her shit when it came time for us to tell Henry which turkey we wanted. She has mentioned something about using 'creative license' a few times, I mean...maybe she's been trying to tell me something."

Beth sat up straighter. "So, you think she may not know about any of the things in the blog? If that was the case, then where are those ideas and recipes coming from...oh my god, Jack...do you think she's poaching this stuff from other sources and claiming them as her own?" Beth's eyes were huge as she said this.

"I don't think so...in my gut, and I've got to feel like my gut is right, but it feels more like I just don't have the full picture...not that she's straight up stealing ideas. At least I don't think so. I want you to know this so that you're prepared for Christmas to not look quite like the photos in *City Meets Country.*

Beth was nodding her head. "No problem. But wow. I had no idea. I mean, I kind of had a funny feeling after Sheila said she didn't think Claire knew what she was doing...it seemed odd, but I let it go. But then there *was* the gingerbread house…and Jack, no offense, but it looks like a ten-year-old made it."

"None taken." He let out a big sigh. "Whatever is going on, it hasn't changed how I feel about her, but it's made me curious as hell…and I hope she feels comfortable enough to confide in me…sooner rather than later."

"She has your heart…doesn't she?" Beth smiled at him.

"She does. I can't put my finger on the exact reasons…but I'm happier when she's around…she makes me feel hopeful and good, if even for only a few more weeks."

"Have you guys talked about what's going to happen when she returns to L.A.?"

Jack shook his head.

"Not at all?" Beth asked, a look of surprise on her face.

"Nope. It seems as if neither of us wants to hear the answers…so we just keep moving forward in silence."

They sat quietly for a few minutes. Archie had resumed his place next to Beth and let out a big snort before closing his eyes.

"She had some interesting ideas for the store, though." Jack relayed to Beth Claire's ideas.

"Jack, that's really kind of brilliant. I think it would work and I think you could do it…with some help. Maybe she could do it…I mean, she could even do it from L.A."

"She said the same thing. And I guess she could…if she even really has those skills though, *right*?" But she must, Jack thought, otherwise why would she have offered to help him?

Jack walked Archie and then made sure Beth had every-thing she needed. Tyler was in Boston again but would be home with lobsters in hand for their annual tradition of a lobster dinner on Christmas Eve.

* * *

EMMY WAS on Claire's phone screen, looking flush in the face as she fanned herself with a magazine.

"Emm, why do you look like you're in a sauna?" Claire asked.

"It's frigg'n ninety degrees out today, but you know my dad, after December first he refuses to turn on the a/c for any reason until after March. I swear Claire, I'm this close to finding my own place." Emmy held her fingers up, her index finger on her thumb.

Claire had heard this several times over the years. Emmy would get frustrated with her family and threaten to move out, but never did. Claire used to be confused by this, but after losing her parents, she no longer questioned Emmy's attachment to her parents and Nona. Things change in an instant, and you can never get them back again.

"I'm sorry…is it going to cool down soon?"

"Nope. We're in the middle of a heat wave…it's supposed to last several more days. I'm wearing shorts and sun dresses…in December. Claire, this is the part where you tell me how freezing you are there in Connecticut."

"It's cold…but no snow yet. I sure hope it snows before I leave."

"Is this normal for them not to have snow yet? I mean, Christmas is only a couple of days away?" Emmy's brows knitted down as she pulled her hair up into a bun off her neck, continuing to fan herself intermittently.

"No, it's not normal. Jack said they always have snow by now. But…," Claire's face broke into a smile, "it's supposed to snow for Christmas."

"That would be beautiful…I have my fingers crossed for you. How'd the turkey brine go…it was easy, right?"

"It seemed okay, actually; I think I got it right. I know I'm no good at any of this, but I'm kind of enjoying myself. And, I feel like I'm really helping them." Claire smiled softly.

"I told you…without me around you've been forced to do these things and *you can do it.*"

"I guess you're right. I can do it." Claire felt slightly triumphant. It was true that as long as Emmy was around, she'd shied away from attempting to make anything. Why would she when her friend was a virtual Martha Stewart?

"How's it going with Jack?" Emmy stopped fanning and gave Claire a serious look. "Have you told him yet?"

Claire let out a visible sigh. "No," she said quietly. "At this point, I figured I'll just wait until after Christmas. No need to spoil the mood at this point.

"You're probably right. How's the popcorn garland going?"

"Pretty good…I'm even adding fresh cranberries to it… I'm nearly finished, and it looks fantastic." She smiled. "Oh shit…I forgot to tell you…remember how Beth wanted a Yule log cake for Christmas Eve to go with their lobster dinner?"

"Yeah," Emmy said slowly.

"I forgot to order one in time at the bakery and now they can't take my order…they're too backed up."

"And…"

"And now I'm going to attempt one myself—" Claire said sheepishly.

"Yikes Claire…that's going to be a challenge. Are you sure you want to take that on?"

"I am. I think I can do it. I've been watching YouTube videos, and I feel confident…our blog on making one was also helpful."

"Okay…call me if you run into difficulties. The trick is to not over bake the cake…if you do, it'll crack when you try to roll it. Are you going to use chocolate or vanilla frosting?"

"Jack and I decided on chocolate."

Emmy raised one eyebrow. "Okay…the chocolate is probably more forgiving. Good luck."

"Thanks. How's Nona?"

"She's good, the increase in her medicine has helped with the dizzy spells. She was feeling good enough to help me bake her biscotti recipe yesterday, even though it was brutal running the oven…they were totally worth it…and we had fun together."

"Oh my god, I love those."

"I know you do…good luck with the cake."

"Thanks…love you."

"Love you back."

After hanging up, Claire pulled up the Yule log blog one more time.

A Christmas Showstopper

I don't know about you, but I love watching the British Baking Show. The final bake of each episode is a grand finale where the bakers create a showstopper. These are wow inducing bakes where the bakers have pulled out all the stops with their creations. That's what a Yule log cake is, a showstopper worthy of your holiday celebration.

The Yule log cake, or Buche de Noel, is the traditional Christmas cake in France, Switzerland, and Belgium. It's a white or chocolate sponge cake layered with buttercream frosting and rolled up to resemble a log which is then frosted with white or chocolate frosting and decorated in any number of ways. If you are feeling especially brave you can make mushrooms out of meringue or add holly leaves and berries…I've even seen woodland creatures such as rabbits or birds added…although this would only be for those of you that are the most experienced of bakers.

Be adventurous and add a little je ne sais quoi to your Christmas by making your own Buche de Noel.

Joyeuses Fetes and Merry Christmas!

She felt confident she could handle this. As she closed her laptop, she heard a knock on her door.

She pulled the front door open to find Jack standing there. "Jack, hi. I wasn't expecting you." She stood back, motioning for him to come in.

"I hope you don't mind. I haven't seen you since the turkey farm. I had hoped to be at Beth's while you were doing the turkey brine, but I got hung up at the store. How'd it go?"

"I think it went well. It's in the fridge in her garage. It'll be ready to bake Christmas morning. I'm going to make the Yule log tomorrow to bring for dinner tomorrow night." She smiled at him.

"Are you sure? I don't want you to be overwhelmed… you've taken on a lot for us…and I can't tell you how much it's meant to me." He took her by the hands and pulled her close. "I mean it Claire; we can pick up a cake at the store. I want you to have fun and not work so hard; Beth will be okay."

She buried her face in his chest. "I'm fine as long as I'm right here…my favorite place to be," she relaxed in his embrace as she snuggled her head against his chest. It *was* her favorite place to be.

CHAPTER 16

*J*ack glanced over at Claire while stopped at the traffic light. They were on their way to Beth's for their annual Christmas Eve lobster dinner. Claire was beautiful in black velvet pants and a red cashmere scoop neck sweater; her scent filled the entire truck. She looked a bit nervous as she clutched onto the cake she'd made.

"What are you thinking about?" He'd grasped one of her hands in his as he drove.

"Oh…I don't know." Claire bit her bottom lip. "I'm excited for Beth to see the garland, I think it turned out nice." She held up a brown bag with one hand. "I guess I'm a bit nervous about the cake. I think it turned out okay…I just hope no one's disappointed."

"I can guarantee you that no one will be disappointed. We're all just grateful for your help, Claire." He glanced over at her as he pulled up in front of Beth's house. "I mean it. Don't worry about a thing, it's going to be great. Plus, we're having lobster for dinner…how much better can it get?" He squeezed her hand. He wanted to reassure her that no one would pass judgment on anything she did. His heart swelled a bit, wanting to protect her.

"Thank you," she said. She leaned over and kissed him. Her lips were soft and warm on his.

There was a tap on the passenger side window. It was Sheila with a big smile on her face as she held up a basket filled with puppies. Pippa was making her way to Beth's porch.

Claire immediately climbed out of the truck. "Oh my god, they're so adorable!"

"Right?!? Pippa did an amazing job," Sheila gushed. "Let's get inside before they get cold. I told Beth and Tyler I'd bring them over today.

Jack and Claire made their way into the house. Sheila had placed the basket of puppies down on the ground. Pippa didn't seem interested at all; she looked like she was on a mom's night out, running freely around the house. Archie, on the other hand, was standing guard next to the basket like a small sentry, occasionally bending down to sniff the three small pups.

"Wow, they are really cute, aren't they?" Jack had kneeled and picked up one of the small black puppies. All three were black with white chests and white toes. Their eyes were open, and their ears were unfolded. Each wore a different color satin ribbon around its neck.

"They need lots of human interaction. So, it's good to hold them a lot." Sheila had grabbed a pup and handed the third one to Beth, who was sitting on the couch.

"I was furious at Archie when this happened, Sheila," Beth said. "But looking at these little cuties, maybe it was meant to be." She beamed as she cuddled the little dog.

After about thirty minutes, Sheila gathered up the puppies and headed back to her house, Pippa reluctantly in tow.

"Hey Jack, give me a hand with this garland." Claire had removed the popcorn and cranberry strand carefully from its bag.

"Sure."

They began to wind it carefully around the tree. Jack bent closer to it and gave it a sniff. "Is this *buttered* popcorn?" His eyebrows dipped as he looked at her.

"Well…yeah…it adds to the Christmas scent," she replied nonchalantly, continuing to drape it on the tree.

"Right, the Christmassy scent of Frankincense and Pop Secret."

"Hey…all they had at the market was the movie theater with butter," she snorted.

Jack laughed to himself. Now that he had a good idea what the real deal was, he found Claire even more adorable. He just wished she would trust him enough to tell him the truth. Hopefully she would soon.

After winding the garland around the tree, they stood back and admired it.

"Claire, it really looks terrific," Jack said. "I'm proud of you." He kissed the top of her head, his hands on her shoulders.

"Thanks…it was really nothing…surprisingly easy, actually."

"I love it! And it smells amazing, Claire," Beth said as she walked into the room, her hands clasped together. "It really completes the tree, thank you so much."

"My pleasure." Claire beamed. "I'm going to put the cake in the refrigerator." She walked off happily.

"Did she use *buttered* popcorn?" Beth whispered to Jack after Claire had left the room; she leaned in, sniffing the garland.

"She said movie theater was the only kind at the store," Jack replied.

"She used *microwave* popcorn?" Beth smiled. "Oh my gosh, the fact that she's trying so hard really warms my heart. She still has said nothing to you?" Beth stood back, one hand on her stomach.

"Nope. Not a word. So, let's just go easy on her. I'm sure she'll say something soon."

* * *

"I CAN HONESTLY SAY that's the first time I've had lobster on Christmas Eve," Claire said, after finishing the sumptuous meal.

"That's a New England holiday for you," Tyler said as he got up and began to clear the table.

"Here, I'll help you," Jack said, getting up and gathering plates. "Beth, you know to stay off your feet; Claire, I want you to take it easy too, you've already done so much." Jack bent down and kissed her on the cheek. He helped Tyler take everything into the kitchen. He was a bit distracted at the moment. He'd noticed Claire on her phone twice. She'd left the room and had been speaking in quiet, hushed tones. Secretive, really. *Could she be talking to her old boyfriend?* Jack had an uneasy feeling in his stomach. He tried to set it aside as he washed dishes.

After he and Tyler got the kitchen somewhat cleaned, Jack put on a pot of coffee and removed the Yule log from the refrigerator. Claire had come in and was rooting around in the fridge, finally pulling out a can of whipped cream.

"The finishing touch," she said as she held the red can in one hand.

Before Jack had figured out what was going on, he might have said something about making freshly whipped cream, but now he knew better. He watched as Claire removed the foil from the cake.

"You need to go to the dining room, so I can surprise you with it." Claire shooed him out of the kitchen.

Jack took his seat at the table. He was worried about the cake, but Claire seemed happy and confident. Beth and Tyler had already downgraded their expectations, so no one would be shocked.

Claire waltzed into the room, setting down the platter with the cake at the center of the table. "Merry Christmas," she said. Her face was beaming as she looked expectantly at everyone.

The cake *was* technically in the shape of a log, but Jack immediately regretted pushing for chocolate frosting. The cake looked more like something Archie would leave on the neighbor's lawn than a Buche de Noel. But when Jack saw the pride in Claire's face, his heart swelled.

"It's beautiful, Claire," he said as he smiled back at her. Even if the cake wasn't the picture perfect one on her blog, it was something that she'd made with her own hands for them and that made it the best cake Jack had ever seen.

Once everyone had a slice of cake and a cup of coffee, Jack took his first bite. It was surprisingly good, *really good*. The exterior might be somewhat of a disaster, but the cake was moist, rich, and delicious.

"Claire, this cake is amazing," said Beth as she leaned back in her chair, savoring the bite. "I mean, it's excellent...such a rich chocolaty flavor and so moist. Yum." Beth dug in for another large bite.

"Thank you," Claire's smile beamed from ear to ear as she enjoyed her creation.

They chatted about football and the expected snow that was supposed to blanket the area overnight before saying good night to Beth and Tyler. They climbed into Jack's truck and headed to Claire's.

"Can I come in and kiss you under the mistletoe?" Jack

said after pulling up in front of the cottage. He leaned over and pulled her into his arms, burying his nose in her hair.

"What if I don't have any mistletoe?" she whispered, as he kissed her neck.

"We'll pretend that you do," he replied, moving from her jaw to her lips.

She wrapped her arms around him and pulled him close. "Sounds good," she whispered.

He came around her side of the truck and helped her out. They walked to the cottage hand in hand. Jack was trying not to think about the clandestine phone calls and the secret he was waiting for her to reveal to him. She'd trust him soon...*right*?

CLAIRE OPENED HER EYES. Jack was still asleep next to her. They'd made love after getting home last night, and once again, it had been wonderful. Claire loved how he made her feel. He had a way of making her feel protected. And the mind-blowing orgasms he gave her didn't hurt. But she worried how he would react once she told him she wasn't really who he thought she was. She'd made a commitment to herself to tell him tonight once they left Beth's. She didn't see any need to bring it up before then, doing so could ruin the day and she didn't want that to happen.

Jack opened his eyes and looked at her. "Merry Christmas," he said, reaching for her.

"Merry Christmas, Jack." Claire slid over so that her naked body was close against his. She rested her head on his chest. This was the special place that, without fail, sent a surge of warmth and happiness through her body. Nothing bad could happen as long as she was in his arms, breathing in his scent.

"Don't you want to see the snow?"

"Snow?" She bolted upright and looked through the window. Everything as far as she could see, was blanketed in a velvety white. "Oh my god, it's so beautiful," she said as she sprung from the bed and slipped on a pair of jeans. "Let's go outside."

"Right now?" Jack sat up slowly, rubbing the sleep from his eyes. "Can't we get coffee first?"

"Let's just go outside for a minute. It's been so long since I've been in the snow, and I've never had a white Christmas before." She pulled him by one arm, dragging him from the bed.

They both dressed warmly before going out into the backyard. The snow was beautiful. It clung to every surface. Tree branches were outlined in white, bushes were blanketed, even the little birdhouse had a layer of snow on its roof.

Claire felt like a little girl. But suddenly she felt overcome with emotion.

"Hey." Jack put his arm around her and pulled her close. "Are you okay?"

Claire bit her lip and nodded her head. "I just miss my parents," she said before the tears fell.

"It's okay," he said as he clung tightly to her. "It's okay."

Claire hoped it *would* be okay.

CHAPTER 17

*C*laire studied her reflection in the bathroom mirror as she dried her hair. She hoped the day went well. She mentally went over her checklist. As soon as they got to Beth's, she needed to get the turkey in the oven. She'd committed Emmy's directions to memory. She felt confident, but nervous at the same time. She also needed to make a salad…that was in her wheelhouse, no problems there. Hank had been a cook in the army and was bringing his "famous" potatoes. She had worried over making gravy, but luckily Jack had volunteered for that. She'd made a mousse the same day she'd made the Yule log. It was currently chilling in the refrigerator. Check, check, and check.

The only hurdle left after the day was over was to come clean to Jack. She was becoming more and more attached to him every day. Going back to Los Angeles was going to be difficult; Claire hadn't spent any time thinking about solutions because there may not be a relationship after Jack learned the truth. She took a deep breath in as she finished drying her hair.

She quickly applied some makeup before getting dressed.

For clothing, she'd opted for a grey cashmere sweater dress, tights, and boots. As she was putting on her earrings Jack poked his head in. "We better get going if we're going to get that turkey cooked." He paused for a minute. "You look fantastic." He came over to her and took her in his arms, kissing her lightly, making Claire desire more. But there was a turkey to cook.

"Yep...we better get going." She smiled at him. "You look pretty handsome yourself." Jack was in dark jeans and a navy-blue sweater; it made his blue eyes stand out; his dark blond hair tousled. He made her insides flip and flop. *I hope he still likes me after tonight.*

* * *

BETH'S HOUSE smelled of Christmas as soon as Claire stepped inside. There was a nice fire going in the fireplace. The house smelled of wood, cinnamon, and Christmas tree. Archie sported a red tartan plaid bow tie. He walked up to Claire and immediately rolled onto his back for a tummy rub, which she obliged. "Merry Christmas, Archie," she said to the small dog.

"Merry Christmas, Tyler." Claire hugged the stocky man.

"How about some coffee guys? Beth's still asleep," Tyler said.

"Sounds good," Jack replied.

They followed Tyler into the kitchen, Claire headed to the garage to pull the turkey from the refrigerator.

"Here, let me grab that," Jack said behind her.

He was always the gentleman, and Claire loved that about him.

After rinsing the brine off the turkey, she tied the legs together, stuffed the cavity with onions and fresh herbs, and then smothered the bird in butter before sliding it into the oven. She smiled to herself as she washed her hands. *I did it.*

She slipped into the other room to quickly call Emmy. Even though it was still early in L.A., Emmy was already up fixing Christmas breakfast for her family.

"Merry Christmas, Emm," Claire said in a whisper, not wanting Jack to hear her on the phone.

"Merry Christmas, Claire," Emmy responded. "Is it a white Christmas?"

"Oh my god, it is. You should see it; it looks like a post-card. I'll send you pictures. But the reason I'm calling, and I gotta keep it quick, I need to know when I should cover the turkey with foil...do I do that now?"

"No—" Emmy replied in a whisper. "—oh, why am *I* whispering, now?" She raised her voice, "you put on the foil once the breast is browned but the turkey still needs some more cooking time."

"Okay," Claire looked up and saw Jack staring at her with a questioning look.

"Okay, now...I'll get that to you, bye," she said loudly before ending the call.

"What was that about?" Jack asked.

"Oh, nothing...just my blog assistant needed the new post to review." *Another lie.*

"Okay...but why were you whispering?" His brows knitted down.

"I didn't want to wake Beth," Claire responded. "Let's go back and finish our coffee." She hooked her arm through his and led him back to the kitchen.

Christmas morning quickly passed into the afternoon. They'd enjoyed a tasty breakfast of bacon and blueberry pancakes, thanks to Tyler. Beth had been up and around before retiring to take a nap. Claire had needed to call Emmy again about the turkey; she was totally confused where to insert the thermometer. She thought maybe Jack had seen her, but maybe not. He'd been acting a bit quiet. Claire figured he was missing his dad this first Christmas without him.

Soon Margie arrived. She was a diminutive octogenarian with snowy white hair perfectly coiffed. She wore a red sweater with a large, enameled Christmas tree broach fastened to it.

"Merry Christmas, dear. You must be Claire," she said as she gave Claire a kiss on the cheek. "Beth said she didn't need me to bring anything, but I brought a fruitcake."

She shoved the tin into Claire's hands; it felt as if it weighed about 5 pounds and probably could be used as a doorstop.

"Thank you, Mrs. Wheeler."

"Call me Margie. No need for formalities, young lady. Now…do you have any eggnog?" Her eyebrows raised and her grey eyes sparkled.

"Sure do, with brandy or without?"

"With, of course, otherwise what would be the point?" she snorted and found a comfortable spot on the couch. Archie immediately jumped up next to her. "Well, hello there, Mr. Archibald…have you been over to see your paramour lately?" Mrs. Wheeler laughed. As she said this, Archie nestled in next to her and let her scratch between his ears.

Tyler walked up to Claire as she was fixing Margie's drink. "Go light on the booze or she'll be talking to the Christmas tree," he whispered.

"Well, ho ho ho, everyone!" Hank had waltzed into the kitchen, his hands and arms loaded down with bags. "Merry Christmas, young lady," he said as he gave Claire a hug. "I'll take one of those eggnogs with the hooch in it." He winked at her. "I've got a big pot here of mashed potatoes, they just need to be reheated on the stove, some more milk stirred into them and then they'll be good to go."

"Thank you, Hank, that really helps a lot." Claire took the pot from one bag and placed in on the stove. She made him an eggnog and set out to find Jack. He was sitting on the porch by himself. Claire sat down next to him. "Are you okay?" she asked, putting a hand on his thigh.

"Yeah. Just thinking." He glanced over at her.

"About your dad?"

"Yeah, and other things...how are you holding up?" he looked at her.

"I'm okay. Being here with your family has helped. It's kept my mind off my parents." She chewed on her bottom lip, stealing a glance at him. It felt like something more was bothering him.

"We better get back in," he said abruptly, standing up. He waited for her to do the same.

"Jack—we really need to talk."

"I know...let's talk about it later," he said. He held his hand out for hers.

* * *

THE REST of the afternoon passed quickly. Soon it was time for dinner. Claire checked over the dining room one last time. She placed the gingerbread house on the buffet, surrounded by pine branches and candles. The table looked festive in reds, greens, and gold. She'd removed the turkey about an hour ago, letting it rest. It looked picture perfect. Just maybe this would all be okay. She was still planning on telling Jack the truth tonight...how he reacted would help her decide what to do next. Her heart ached for it to be okay. The thought of no longer being with him was unbearable.

"Okay everyone, it's time for dinner," Tyler called out.

Jack and Claire finished bringing all the food to the table. It was a beautiful Christmas feast.

Beth's face beamed when she saw it. "Oh my gosh," she said, taking her seat. "Dad would be proud." She reached over and grabbed Jack's hand. Tears had formed in her eyes. "I miss him so much."

"Me too," Jack said, taking his sister's hand.

"We all do," replied Hank. "Here's to Harry." He raised his glass. Everyone held theirs up also.

"Well...let's get started," Jack said. He sliced turkey for everyone while they passed around the side dishes. "Everything looks great."

"It sure does. Thanks again Claire for helping. I feel as if you're part of the family now," Beth said. She smiled at Claire before looking over at Jack, who glanced away.

Claire looked down at her plate, the turkey looked great. She was so proud of herself. *I did it.* She took a bite, and her taste buds immediately recoiled. *Oh my god, it tastes like a salt lick.* She quickly glanced around the table and saw everyone's faces in various stages of surprise.

"The, uh, turkey tastes like salt," Hank said, pulling it from his mouth into his napkin. "Better not eat that with my high blood pressure, liable to end up in the hospital."

Claire looked at Jack. "It's uh...*kind of* edible." A look of discomfort was on his face as he attempted to chew the turkey.

"I don't understand what went wrong." Claire's heart had dropped into her stomach.

"I think the brine had too much salt," Beth said, a sympathetic look on her face. "How much did you put in?"

"I don't remember," Claire felt panic take over. She could feel her emotions rising, threatening to start an army of tears rolling. "I followed the recipe...salt, sugar, garlic, oranges—"

"Wait...where did you get the sugar from?" Beth asked, her eyes wide.

Claire felt confused. "From the blue cannister in the pantry, the one marked 'sugar.'"

"Oh my god, Claire it's my fault...that's salt in there, I should have told you...even though it says 'sugar' on the label, I keep my pickling salt in there...so the brine was all salt and no sugar. Oh...don't cry, Claire, it's not your fault. You did a great job."

Jack had put his arm around Claire. "It's *not* your fault, a simple mix up because this isn't your kitchen...don't look so sad."

But Claire *was* sad.

Just then, the faint sound of glass tinkling against glass was heard coming from the living room, along with the sound of rustling tree branches. Everyone had gone quiet as they all listened to the sound.

"What's *that*?" Beth said.

"Where's that pooch?" Hank asked.

"Oh no, Archie...no..." Jack quickly got up and ran to the living room, Claire was right behind him. They made it into the room just in time to see Archie, the popcorn garland in his mouth, pull the entire Christmas tree down to the ground, sending up a loud crash of glass hitting the floor. The dog trotted off to his bed with his prize in his mouth.

"Oh no!" Claire cried out, her hands on her cheeks. She couldn't believe what she'd just witnessed. And now the living room was one big mess, the eight-foot tree felled by one small dog. Broken ornaments and tree branches were strewn everywhere. "This is awful...I just—"

"Your gingerbread house just collapsed." Hank yelled from the dining room.

"Yeah, looks like it was in the 1906 quake," Margie added.

Claire could no longer stop the torrent of tears that were

waiting to breach the flood gates. "I'm such a fraud, and now I've ruined your Christmas," she sobbed.

"Christmas isn't ruined," Jack said, putting his arms around her.

Claire was nodding her head as tears continued to pour out. "And Tom...I'm so sorry Tom," she said in between heaving sobs.

"Tom? Who's Tom?" Jack asked as he looked at her.

Claire let out another wail.

"Is that who you've been on the phone with?" Jack's eyes narrowed as he held her shoulders.

"What?" she said, wiping her eyes.

"Who's Tom, Claire?" He was sounding upset now.

She looked up at him, her chest shuddering as she breathed in. "Tom the turkey...he died in vain." More sobs heaved out.

"If Tom's the turkey, then who've you been on the phone with all day?" Jack's eyes were questioning hers.

Claire sniffled. "Emmy. She's been helping me. I'm a phony Jack. Not a single thing in *City Meets Country* is made by me...it's all made by Emmy, my friend. I only *write* the blog and take the pictures."

"I thought you had been on the phone with your ex-boyfriend."

"What? *Zachary*? No...just Emmy, she's been trying to help me through all this...I haven't done any of the things I write about."

Jack looked at her, his eyes kind. "I know," he said softly.

"You know?" Claire looked up at him. He was nodding his head. "How long have you known?" Hope flooded through her body.

"Since sometime between the gingerbread house and the turkey farm," he said. He pulled her into his chest. He smelled good, and she felt safe against him.

"Are you mad?" She cautiously looked up at him.

"No. I'm not mad. I just wished you would have trusted me with the truth sooner." He ran one hand over her hair, smoothing it down.

"I thought that you'd fallen for the *fake* Claire...I was afraid to tell you." She chewed on her bottom lip.

"I fell for the *real* Claire, the one right here in my arms. The one that loves baseball and reads x-rated romance novels to senior citizens. The one that understands what I'm going through. The one that despite knowing her shortcomings tried to help us and did. And the one that's adorable as hell. *That's* the Claire I fell for." He pulled her closer and brought his lips to hers, kissing her slowly and deeply.

Applause broke out around them. Everyone had been frozen in their tracks, listening to the entire exchange.

Claire glanced from face to face. Everyone was beaming and happy. And so was she.

CHAPTER 18

*E*veryone gathered in the living room to exchange gifts. The ornament-free tree, with its busted branches, was back up in its stand thanks to Jack and Tyler. Claire had helped sweep up the mess from the floor. Archie had made a big huff when Tyler took the garland away from him. The small dog retired to his bed for the rest of the day, refusing to look at anyone.

"This is for you, Claire." Beth handed her a small box. In it was a pair of earrings, delicate beads of glass hung from sterling silver.

"They're beautiful Beth, thank you."

"A woman here in town made them; she's really quite talented. I hope you enjoy them."

"I will, thank you again…you really didn't have to get me anything." Claire said.

"Don't be silly. I wanted to, you've been so helpful, and I wanted to show you how much I appreciate everything you've done." Beth smiled at her.

Claire handed a large gift box to Beth. "It's for the baby."

Inside was a small quilt adorned with tiny, embroidered Scottie dogs along the border.

"I love it...it's perfect. I'm sure these dogs will be better behaved than Archie," Beth laughed.

Archie lifted his head and snorted at the sound of his name.

"Here young lady, I gotcha a little something." Hank pressed a gift bag into Claire's hands.

"Hank...how sweet. I feel bad that I didn't get you anything," Claire said as she pulled out the tissue paper wrapped item.

"You may not feel bad anymore once you see what it is," he said, a mischievous grin on his face.

Claire laughed as she pulled out a Red Sox baseball cap. "You're right...I don't feel bad anymore...seriously though, thank you." She gave him a big hug, which caused Hank's cheeks to turn red.

"Here Jack. This is for you, from me." Claire handed him a present.

Jack pulled the ribbon from the package and opened the box. He pulled out a beautiful silver frame. In it was a picture of him and his dad at Fenway.

"Beth gave me the picture," Claire said softly.

"I love it, thank you." He gave her a big hug and a kiss.

"For you." Jack handed Claire a large box.

She was nervous as she pulled back the tissue paper. She gasped when she saw what was inside. It was a birdhouse made as an exact replica of the cottage, complete with a stone chimney, shutters, and even a small wreath hung on the door. "Jack...I love it."

"Something to remember River Falls by," he replied.

Claire got a pit in her stomach; she would only be in town for a bit longer and then she'd be back in Los Angeles. She really didn't want to leave Jack or River Falls.

* * *

It was late once Jack and Claire made it back to her house. As soon as they got through the front door, they were tangled up in one another's arms. Lips on lips, hands roaming over each other's bodies. Claire moaned as Jack's tongue found hers. She pulled off her coat and threw it to the floor, Jack followed suit. They stopped only to unlace and remove their boots before embracing again.

He ran his lips over her neck, kissing every square inch. Claire's insides had turned to warm mush as he made his way once again to her mouth. He softly brushed his lips against hers while pulling her body tight against him. He let out a groan and removed the rest of his clothing, and Claire did the same. They made their way back to the bedroom, leaving a trail of discarded clothing behind them.

In a second, Jack had Claire on the bed, kissing her jaw and making his way down to her breasts. She ran her fingers through his hair as every nerve ending in her body lit up. His warm mouth trailed down her stomach and eventually found the area between her thighs. She moaned as soon as his tongue reached her most sensitive area.

"Oh my god, Jack, that feels so good," she said in a low voice. She closed her eyes as he worked his tongue and mouth on her, soon making her feel that most pleasant sensation rip through her entire body.

He held her gaze before bringing his lips to hers, allowing her to taste herself on him. Claire could feel his desire hard against her. "Claire," he moaned as he buried his face in her neck. He suddenly stopped and looked up at her. "Shit. I don't have a condom…I'll have to run over to my place to grab one. Shit, shit, shit."

Claire reached a hand up to his cheek. "I've got us covered. I picked some up just in case this happened."

"You did? Oh my god, you're awesome. Where are they?"

"In the nightstand drawer." She continued to run her hands over his cheek and through his hair. Claire felt about as good as she could right now but wanted more. She wanted to feel him inside her…his warmth filling her up.

Jack leaned over and pulled the drawer open. Claire noticed a small grin on his face.

"What? What's making you smile?" she asked playfully.

"Um…I think I found your flashlight."

"What? Oh my god… *how embarrassing*." Her cheeks were burning red hot.

He smoothed the hair from her forehead. "Nothing to be embarrassed about…it's part of what I love about you… you're always surprising me."

"You *love* something about me?" Just the mention of the 'L' word made her stomach fill with butterflies. She searched his eyes for clues.

"I do. Actually, I love everything about you." He paused as he looked at her. "I love you, Claire."

Claire felt her heart soar. *He loves me.* She smiled from ear to ear, her embarrassment forgotten. "I love you too, Jack."

With those words Jack slid one arm under her shoulders and neck, he leaned his body against hers as he gently kissed her lips. He was warming every inch of her, and Claire couldn't get enough of him. She pressed her nose into his neck, inhaling his scent. She felt exhilaration from the tips of her toes to the top of her head. Jack slowly entered her, causing her to take a breath in. They moved as one until Jack moaned her name softly.

Afterwards, they laid together. Claire curled up against him, his arms around her felt warm and protective. She was in love, and she couldn't be happier. But…they needed to figure out how to make this all work. *But how?*

* * *

OVER THE NEXT WEEK, Jack and Claire were inseparable. They spent their days having fun in the snow. Jack taught her how to cross-country ski and she loved it. It was exhilarating to be out in an untouched blanket of white snow. It was peaceful and beautiful.

They spent one afternoon building a family of snowmen, adorning them with scarves and hats. Jack had even made a little Scottie dog snowman for Beth, complete with a red tartan plaid scarf. Archie gave it one look and snorted before trotting off.

They had dinner with Beth and Tyler on several nights and made several trips to visit the puppies to help socialize them. Sheila said she was keeping one but needed to find a home for the other two. She stared at Jack until he put up his hands.

"No...not me, Sheila. What am I going to do with two puppies? Have you talked to Beth?"

"She's having a baby, Jack...she won't have time for puppies."

He looked at Claire and Claire looked back at him. She knew what he was thinking, but she was going back to L.A. in a few days...she couldn't take care of puppies either. Speaking of returning, she and Jack hadn't worked out anything definite yet, only that they were going to try a bi-coastal relationship and see how it went. Claire wasn't happy with the idea, and she was pretty sure Jack wasn't either. But they enjoyed their days without bringing the subject up too much. And they enjoyed their nights. They made love as often as they could. Claire was trying to imprint the feel of his body to her memory to hold her through the weeks, or even months, until she would see him again.

Finally, the day she was leaving arrived. She'd woken up

that morning with a heavy heart as she inhaled his scent while they lay in bed together.

"What time do you need to leave by?" Jack asked as he kissed her head, his arms wrapped tightly around her.

"By eleven. I'm all packed, so we can have a leisurely morning. She looked up at him and smiled.

"Does that mean what I think it means?" he pulled her closer.

She nodded her head. "It does."

They made love one last time before reluctantly getting out of bed. Jack made Claire a breakfast of pancakes and coffee. They sat quietly, stealing glances at each other as they ate.

"I wish I could drive you to the airport," Jack said, putting the last of her suitcases into her car.

"I have to return my rental, plus I would be a crying wreck. Better to say goodbye here so that I have time to pull it together." Her bottom lip quivered as she said this. Jack pulled her in tight. Hugging her as if his life depended on it. Claire didn't want it to end. Ever.

They kissed for what seemed like forever before Claire untangled herself. "I better get going."

"All the roads should be plowed, but drive carefully," Jack said as he closed the driver's side door. "Call me if you run into any trouble. I'll be there in a flash." He kissed her one last time.

Claire pulled out of the driveway of the little cottage. She saw Jack waving in her rear-view mirror. She was leaving a place and a man that had made her very happy. A place and a man who'd helped her heal over the loss of her parents. She was leaving her heart behind. She drove off, leaving River Falls with tears in her eyes and a heart that felt as if it was missing most of what it needed to survive.

* * *

JACK HEADED to the store with a heavy heart. With Claire officially gone it felt as if a dark cloud had rolled into his life. His sunshine was missing. Claire had stolen his heart. She'd been someone to listen to his feelings of grief over the loss of his father. She'd also listened empathetically as he shared his feelings of guilt over the death of Private Martinez. She'd held him and told him it wasn't his fault, but that she understood why he felt the way he did. Claire encouraged him to seek counseling at the VA, to work his way through his feelings. It was sound advice that he planned to follow up on.

But for now, he needed to figure out how to implement the plans for Wilson's Hardware that they'd discussed. He pulled into his parking spot at the back of the store and headed in.

"Howdy," Hank said. He was assembling the new battery display. "How'd it go?" He looked at Jack with concern in his eyes.

"Fine. I guess." Jack didn't really want to talk about it. "Hey, that one looks better than the old one." He nodded towards the new set up.

"Yeah...it's bigger...we can keep more stock on it," Hank said.

"I'm going to be in the back...just give me a holler if you need me," Jack called out to him as he disappeared into his office in the back. He didn't feel sociable, and besides, he needed to get out emails to the web designers Claire had recommended.

She had also suggested that they use a small part of the store as an artisan co-op. She'd suggested contacting the woman who'd made her earrings, the person she'd found the quilt from, along with some other contacts Beth had suggested. People could use the storefront in which to sell their handmade items. Jack would only charge a small percent of the sales from it. The main point would be that it would bring traffic through the door.

Claire had also suggested seeing if Jenny wanted to open a small coffee bar inside the store. It could be for to-go coffee orders; another way to bring business into the store and keep it there as people sipped on a coffee drink and browsed. These ideas, along with the kits for birdhouses, doll houses, and playhouses, were all brilliant and doable. Claire had even offered to write blog posts for him. He just wished she would be here in person. Things would not be the same without her around.

He got to work sending out the emails and then he got to work drafting plans for the birdhouses along with a list of products needed to construct them. He'd been so absorbed with his work over the past couple of hours that he didn't notice Hank standing in the doorway.

"Jack...I've been calling your name," he said excitedly. "Dodger cap is here."

Great. Another out-of-town Dodger fan for Hank to argue with. "Okay...try not to scare them away. And please, don't get into a discussion whether Clemens was better than Koufax...I'm telling you, that's a loser."

"No. I mean *your* Dodger cap is here." Hank beamed as he rocked back on his heels, his hands stuffed into his pockets.

Jack jumped up. "Claire? Claire's here?" *Oh my god, did something happen? Is she okay?* He rushed out to the front of the store and there she was. And just like that, his world was bright once again. "Claire, are you okay? What are you doing here? Did you miss your flight?" He'd put his hands on her shoulders, rubbing them as he searched her eyes.

She just smiled at him. "Nope, none of those things. I just couldn't do it, Jack."

"Do what?" he asked, as a feeling of happiness drenched his entire being.

"I couldn't leave you or River Falls." She threw her arms around him. "I just couldn't."

Jack pulled her tight as he hugged her.

"I contacted Roger Drake about the cottage; he said it's mine for as long as I want it."

"You're staying?" he asked.

"I'm staying." She beamed at him, leaning closer and kissing him softly. I hope you want me to."

"Are you kidding? You do not know how badly I want you to." He kissed her back for a long moment before finally pulling himself away from her soft lips.

"What about your blog? And Emmy?"

"Emmy and I talked for a long time. She helped me work this all out. We came up with an idea that allows me to stay in River Falls."

"I'm so glad that you're back." Jack pulled her close and kissed her. He never wanted to be without her. Ever.

"*J*ack, hold still," Claire said with exasperation, her camera in her hand. "Really...why is this so hard for you?"

Jack was wearing jeans and a white t-shirt; he had a saw in one hand and was balancing a piece of wood on a sawhorse with the other. "Because I feel ridiculous, that's why."

Hank let out a snort.

"Don't even start, Hank." Jack said.

"Not saying a word," Hank replied as he chuckled under his breath.

"Really, Claire...is this necessary?"

"Jack...Emmy is going to feature you in next month's *City Meets Country* blog, and on all of its social media platforms, including Instagram...which has half a million followers alone...ninety-nine percent of whom are women...a picture of a hot guy holding a saw will go viral...traffic to your website will explode. That's why."

Emmy had slowly taken over the reins of the blog. At first, it was hard for her to put herself out there, as her shyness got in the way. But once she wrote a few posts of her own, she took to it brilliantly. She'd even added a style section, focusing on fashions for curvy figures. The response to it was phenomenal. The Instagram account alone gained an additional fifty thousand followers in just a few months.

Claire had let go of the blog completely, which allowed her to focus her attention one hundred percent on getting Wilson's Hardware's website and social media up and running.

"Okay," Jack grumbled. "But we need to wrap it up soon... Beth needs us to walk Archie."

Claire took a few more pictures before looking up from her camera. "Is Tyler out of town again?"

"He is. She's got her hands full."

As it turned out, Beth *had* been carrying twins. Little Amelia had been hiding behind her brother, Oliver. When, during her delivery, the doctor had announced there was a second baby, Beth had cried out: "See, it wasn't the ice cream making me fat," before quickly sobering up to the fact that she now had *two* newborns to care for and bursting into tears. Everyone had wondered whether she was elated or frightened. Probably both.

Tyler's mom had stayed with them for the first three months; since then, Claire and Jack pitched in whenever they could, especially when Tyler was away on business.

"That's fine. The pups need a walk anyway...they'll enjoy seeing their dad. I'll go get them; I think we're done here."

Claire walked out to the front of the store, where a makeshift pen was set up for the puppies. Once Claire had decided to stay, she and Jack offered to take two of Pippa's puppies. Finley and Scout jumped around when they saw Claire, letting out small yips. They both sported tartan plaid collars around their necks.

"I know...you guys are so excited to go see Archie...

c'mon." She scooped the two pups into her arms, immediately being covered by kisses. She smiled as she watched Jack walk over to her. He leaned down and kissed her tenderly on the lips before letting the pups give him their kisses. Things couldn't have gone better since she'd made River Falls her home.

She and Jack had traveled to Los Angeles together last month, closing the sale of her parent's townhome. It had been emotional for Claire to move everything out of the home she'd shared with them. Jack had been rock-solid in his support of her.

She had introduced him to Emmy and Emmy's family. Nona took a shine to him and was continually trying to feed him. It had been an enjoyable time and Claire was happy that Jack and Emmy had bonded.

She'd also taken him to meet Ruthie and to say goodbye to her. She still read to Ruthie once a week via Zoom. Ruthie was still on her super steamy romcom kick. Claire also took Jack to all her favorite spots. They'd walked on the beach in Santa Monica, ate street tacos and pho, and even took in a Dodgers' game; Jack had insisted on decking himself out in Red Sox gear even though they weren't playing. He got a few comments, but not too bad considering that Boston wasn't well loved in Los Angeles.

She made the bold decision to offer to buy the cottage from Roger Drake and his siblings. At first, they hadn't been too interested in selling. But Claire made them an offer they couldn't turn down. Jack moved out of the small house he had been renting and moved in with her. With Scout and Finley, they were a happy foursome. Claire had to pinch herself some days. Life in River Falls with Jack made her whole; it made her happy. *Really* happy.

. . .

ELEVEN AND A HALF MONTHS LATER:

Claire pushed her toes into the warm white sand. She tilted her head back and soaked up the heat of the sun above her. No matter how many days she would soak up the warmth, it didn't feel as if her bones would ever completely thaw out from the New England winters.

"Pina Colada time." Jack's voice cut through her reverie. He set a frosty cold glass topped with a cherry and a slice of pineapple down on the table next to her.

"Pretty soon I'm going to turn into a Pina Colada," Claire said as she took a sip of the creamy white concoction.

"You would be the cutest Pina Colada ever," he said before leaning over and kissing her on the cheek. "Let's stay here until sunset...I'll run over to Bailey's Beach Hut and grab us another drink and some munchies to watch the sunset with."

Claire looked over at him. His body was already tan from the week of sun. He looked great in his navy-blue swim trunks. They would be here for another week, and then it was back to the bitter cold. This was Claire's second winter in River Falls and she still couldn't get her body's thermostat to switch over from its Los Angeles setting. But it was worth it. Shoot, she'd even move to the North Pole if it meant being with Jack. She loved him with all her heart, and the love and affection she got in return was more than she could ever hope for. He was a tender and sexy lover, a companion to have fun with, and the best shoulder to lean on that she'd ever met. He turned out to be perfect for her.

Together they had gotten the store to turn a profit. Wilson's Hardware had a fantastic following on their blog, which was driven by Claire's adept hand at their social media accounts. She'd designed branding and a logo, simply using the initials "WH" in black against a robin's egg blue oval background. The store was selling kits for doll houses, bird houses, and playhouses like hotcakes. They could barely keep up with the demand.

They'd also added an artisan co-op to one corner of the store. In exchange for a small percent of the sales, many locals were selling their crafts in the store and on their website. Claire was astounded at the beautiful items: hand-made beeswax candles and soaps, knitted scarfs, caps and mittens, quilts, jewelry, and, of course, Jack's bird houses.

The increased foot traffic was also boosted by Jenny's small coffee stand located inside the store. Many different types of tea and coffee drinks were available, as well as some bakery items. Jack added a couple of small sofas and tables to the area, and it quickly became a gathering spot. During the warmer months, there was seating outdoors. The profit from all these changes meant that Jack and Beth could continue their father's legacy.

"It's up!" Claire exclaimed excitedly, gesturing towards her iPad.

"Read it to me," Jack said. He'd put his sunglasses on and laid his head back for optimal sun exposure.

"Okay," Claire replied. She read the new blog post aloud to him.

A WEDDING in Connecticut by Emmy Parsons

It's official...our Claire Bennett is now Claire Bennett-Wilson. She and Jack tied the knot on the Saturday following Christmas. It was a beautiful and magical winter wedding. Can I say right now that winter weddings are the most beautiful! Especially when set against the backdrop of snow-covered Connecticut; it was absolutely breathtaking.

The bride wore an off-white satin sheath style dress topped with a silver fur shawl (faux, of course!) wrapped around her shoulders. Her hair piled up in a romantic updo. The bridesmaids, including moi as maid of honor, wore deep red velvet dresses. Claire held a beautiful bouquet of red and white cabbage roses with sprigs of green spruce all wrapped in satin.

Jack made a handsome, picture perfect (and yes...there is a link to the pictures below) groom in a traditional black tuxedo with silvery grey accents. The groomsmen in matching tuxedos as well. And of course, the dogs! Little Finley and Scout were on their best behavior, and they looked completely adorable in red velvet collars with small white cabbage roses adorning them.

The reception was held at the River Falls' Inn, a charming building that's on the historic register. Before dinner, there was a reception with servers passing around silver trays with flutes of champagne and hors d'oeuvres of Brie wrapped in phyllo, oysters on the half shell, and lobster with gruyere in puff pastry.

The sit-down dinner was heavenly. The room was lit with beautiful crystal chandeliers, the white cloth-covered tables had been adorned with pine wreaths, dotted with red holly berries, with white candles at their centers. Dinner was Beef Wellington with pureed potatoes and roasted winter vegetables.

And last, but not least, the wedding cake! It was five layers of rich chocolate cake, iced in white frosting, with piped green spruce branches and red berries decorating the sides. Creamy custard and tart raspberry preserves filled the layers of sponge. The best part was the custom-made cake topper of a bride wearing a Dodgers' cap and a groom in a Red Sox cap...it was simply adorable.

The lovely couple is now off soaking up the Caribbean sun for the next two weeks. Congratulations to Claire and Jack...here's to a long and happy marriage.

The End

Want to read Emmy's story next? Pre-Order now on Amazon. The book will be released on 12/15/2022.

AFTERWORD

Dear reader,

I want to thank you for taking the time to read "A Christmas in Connecticut." I hope you enjoyed reading it as much as I enjoyed writing it. For indie authors, reviews from readers are critical to a book's success. If you enjoyed this book, kindly leave a review at: Amazon. It would be greatly appreciated.

I am currently finishing Emmy's story in "A Christmas in New York" which will be available December 15, 2022. It's a grumpy/sunshine story and I know you'll love it as much as I do. You can pre-order now on Amazon.

You can stay updated by joining my mailing list on my website: www.emilyfrenchbooks.com

Happy reading,

Emily

ABOUT THE AUTHOR

Emily French is a former family law attorney. She was born and raised in the San Francisco Bay Area. She now resides in North Carolina with her husband and their two dogs who are welcome and sometimes unwelcome distractions. When she's not writing, she can be found reading, cooking, traveling, or watching baseball.

Visit her website at EmilyFrenchBooks.com

ALSO BY EMILY FRENCH

Made in the USA
Middletown, DE
27 November 2022

16195950R00104